LITTLE DAVID

AND HIS

GOLIATHS

JERRY REYNOLDS

Gotham Books
30 N Gould St.
Ste. 20820, Sheridan, WY 82801
https://gothambooksinc.com/
Phone: 1 (307) 464-7800

Published by Gotham Books (July 29, 2022)

ISBN: 978-1-956349-62-7 (sc)
ISBN: 978-1-956349-63-4 (e)

Because of the dynamic nature of the Internet, any web addresses or links contained in this book may have changed since publication and may no longer be valid.

The views expressed in this work are solely those of the author and do not necessarily reflect the views of the publisher, and the publisher hereby disclaims any responsibility for them

In every generation there are some who are big dreamers.

They are not satisfied with their current situation. In Kerala, India, during the 1950's and 60's, men were willing to leave their home and look for better paying jobs in bigger cities like Mumbai and Chennai. Later, the rush was towards the middle eastern countries and after that towards the North America.

I am inspired by the stories of these great men who were willing to sacrifice anything for a better life for them and their families.

This book is dedicated to all the fathers and husbands who sacrificed their comfortable home life to build a better future for the next generations to come

Table of Contents

Chapter 1 7

Chapter 2 14

Chapter 3 20

Chapter 4 27

Chapter 5 34

Chapter 6 41

Chapter 7 48

Chapter 8 55

Chapter 9 62

Chapter 10 69

Chapter 11 75

Chapter 12 81

Chapter 13 88

Chapter 14 96

Chapter 15 103

Chapter 16 109

Chapter 17 116

Saul said to David, "Go, and the LORD be with you."

38Then Saul dressed David in his own tunic. He put a coat of armor on him and a bronze helmet on his head.39 David fastened on his sword over the tunic and tried walking around because he was not used to them.

"I cannot go in these," he said to Saul, "because I am not used to them." So, he took them off. 40Then he took his staff in his hand, chose five smooth stones from the stream, put them in the pouch of his shepherd's bag and, with his sling in his hand, approached the Philistine.

41Meanwhile, the Philistine, with his shield bearer in front of him, kept coming closer to David. 42He looked David over and saw that he was little more than a boy, glowing with health and handsome, and he despised him. 43He said to David, "Am I a dog, that you come at me with sticks?" And the Philistine cursed David by his gods. 44"Come here," he said, "and I'll give your flesh to the birds and the wild animals!"

45David said to the Philistine, "You come against me with sword and spear and javelin, but I come against you in the name of the Lord Almighty, the God of the armies of Israel, whom you have defied. 46This day the Lord will deliver you into my hands, and I'll strike you down and cut off your head. This very day I will give the carcasses of the Philistine army to the birds and the wild animals, and the whole world will know that there is a God in Israel. 47All those gathered here will know that it is not by sword or spear that the Lord saves; for the battle is the Lord's, and he will give all of you into our hands."

[48]As the Philistine moved closer to attack him, David ran quickly toward the battle line to meet him. [49]Reaching into his bag and taking out a stone, he slung it and struck the Philistine on the forehead. The stone sank into his forehead, and he fell facedown on the ground.

[50]So, David triumphed over the Philistine with a sling and a stone; without a sword in his hand he struck down the Philistine and killed him.

[51]David ran and stood over him. He took hold of the Philistine's sword and drew it from the sheath. After he killed him, he cut off his head with the sword.

When the Philistines saw that their hero was dead, they turned and ran. [52]Then the men of Israel and Judah surged forward with a shout and pursued the Philistines to the entrance of Gath53 and to the gates of Ekron.

-1 Samuel 17 (The Holy Bible)

Chapter 1

Kochu Daveed (Little David) was born in the small town of Kochi, in the State of Kerala, in South India. He was the second child of Kavungal Pathro and his wife Mariamma. The history of Kavungal family can be traced back to the ancient times of Kochi. A long time ago, Kochi was a small fishing village. Small groups of fishermen used to go fishing together in one boat and gradually formed a part of a group with a strong leader guiding them. The leader was called *Mooppan* (Chieftain) at that time, as a mark of respect for his leadership. The power of Mooppans grew steadily and within three to four generations they almost had full control over the group. The Mooppan's family began to own the largest fleet of fishing vessels and they controlled the employment, cash disbursal, and sales. They started acquiring more land for their personal use and building bigger houses.

One of the Mooppans bought a large plot of land near *Kavu* (sacred groves). *Sarpa Kavu* (meaning Abode of Snakes) is a sacred space seen near traditional homes in Kerala. The site is believed to be inhabited by snakes, and the area usually has a stone statue of Naga Raja (King of the Snakes) and other Naga Devatas (snake deities), where offerings and rites are performed during special ceremonies. This is a Hindu ritual performed by certain sects of Namboothiris (Brahmins), and all castes hold the *Sarpa Kavu* in reverence, with access forbidden to the area unless for ceremonies.

Thus, their family was given the name as Kavungal, meaning near the Kavu. During the thirteenth century, Kochi began to be known as a port town due to its natural harbor, and ships from far and wide came in to trade in spices. Most of the coastal town of Kochi by that time was under the influence of Christianity, and so meat and wine were easily available for the sailors, which made it an important port for replenishing their food storage.

One of the enterprising and daring young bloods in the Kavungal family, Kochu Ouseph, decided to let go of their traditional fishing ancestry and ventured in with the shipping companies to supply fresh meat to the visiting ships. By the time Kochu Daveed's great-grandfather, Kavungal Vareed took over the business, they were the largest Clearing and Forwarding agents in Kochi. Kavungal Vareed had two sons, who inherited the business. The eldest, Kavungal Daveed, had only two daughters, who were married off to other rich families. The youngest, Kavungal Migayel, had four sons and two daughters. Kavungal Pathro was the youngest of them and the most notorious. Though each one of the sons had their own homes, they worked together in their family business. There was unity and success in that. Except for Pathro, each one of the men in the family worked for the common success of the business.

Pathro was of a different nature. He would come to the office in the morning, not for work, but to get some money from the elders and go out with his friends. He enjoyed the full life of a bachelor. Being the youngest and everyone's favorite, no one tried to force him to work. As per the belief of that time, everyone thought that he would be more responsible when he gets married to some good girl from a respectable family. So his father started to look for a good alliance for his young wayward son. One of his cousins brought in good news about a beautiful girl from her village. As per the customs in the family, a date was arranged for a formal visit to the girl's house by the elders of the would-be groom's family. Pathro was not allowed to go along. He was allowed to go and see the girl only if the elders of the family approved the girl's family. Everything went well as per custom. When Pathro went to see the girl along with his elder brother, he liked the girl, her family, and the vast paddy fields they owned at that time. He got along well with the younger brother of the girl whom he found to be of the same nature as him.

The wedding of Kavungal Pathro and Mariamma was a very big event in Kochi. The marriage function took place at the bride's parish church. The Bishop of Alappuzha solemnized the wedding. The bride and groom went home on a beautifully decorated cart driven by white horses. Since the bride was from a rich farming family, the whole village was invited to the wedding. All kinds of meat and vegetable dishes, prepared by famous chefs, were served at the banquet after the wedding. The newlyweds stayed there in the bride's house for three nights as per custom and then returned to Kochi. The reception given to them in Kochi was done in such a grand manner as that not before seen there. The reception party went on and on till the wee hours of the morning and by the time Pathro took leave from his friends and entered his room, the bride was already asleep in one corner of the bed. He did not disturb her but went and slept on the other side of the bed till the afternoon of the next day.

When the bride woke up the next morning, she saw her husband sleeping peacefully on one side of the bed. She got up immediately and went out in search of her mother-in-law. Thus began the new life for Mariamma in Kochi. She was totally the opposite of her husband in looks and behavior. While Pathro was tall and broad, she was short and tiny. She was very timid and soft-spoken while Pathro was boisterous and loud. Despite these differences they were a loving couple and he was enamored with her. He started taking his life more seriously and began to take interest in the business. His family thought that their plan worked well and his father was happy to see the changes in him. He began to spend the evenings at home with his beautiful wife and all went well until the birth of their first child.

As per the custom of the place, Mariamma was taken to her parent's house for her childbirth on her seventh month of pregnancy. She returned only when the child was 6 months old. Their first child was a girl and they decided to stay there for a long time because it was the first grandchild of her household and her parents kept forcing her to stay more time with them. She couldn't resist their loving demands and in turn, forced Pathro to spend more time in her house. Pathro enjoyed the special attention he got at his in-law's house. The youngest brother-in-law became his good friend and they both spent most of the time drinking coconut and palm toddy and enjoying the rich farmer's life.

Pathro began to go back to his old ways and the old friends who had abandoned him when he became a responsible husband, flocked back to him. He stopped taking care of the business and seeing this his brothers decided to give him a small share of the profits, just to maintain his lifestyle. By the time he had four kids, three girls and a boy, he had sold all his share of the family business to his brothers and was content with taking care of his coconut plantations.

When Kochu Daveed , son of Pathro, was ten years old, his father had sold most of the land to maintain his lifestyle and they had only the house and the surrounding plot of land of about half an acre left. His uncles and cousins kept a distance from them. The only thing that prevented them from starvation was the regular supply of rice and coconuts from his mother's house. Mariamma's parents and brothers did their best to support her, but they too were going through a bad time. Her younger brother fell in love with the local toddy shop owner's daughter and was forced to marry her when she got pregnant. This made them lose face in the community and they had to partition their property so that their youngest son could live separately with his low-caste wife. With the split in their income, they found it difficult to maintain the steady flow of supplies to Mariamma's house. This stopped completely when her parents died one after another within a year and her elder brother, being a sick person himself, decided that it was time to take care of his own family first.

By the age of eleven, Kochu Daveed had learned some of the hard facts of life. He understood that poverty means loneliness. Poverty does not have relatives. If you are poor, you are not welcome in any of the houses of your rich relatives. Some days they might feel generous enough to call you to their houses to give you some much-needed food, but even then, you are not allowed to enter their houses through the front door. You enter through the back door, receive whatever is being offered and then exit through the same back door.

Daveed learned that food is one of the basic needs in life. Nothing else matters if one is hungry. By the Grace of God, air and water are free in this world, shelter, and clothing to cover the shame is provided by the parents but getting enough food for the day was a great feat for him. His father had stopped taking care of his family. He watched his father go out early in the morning to meet his friends, after sipping his customary black tea from the hands of his mother, wearing his white mundu and kurta, hair combed well and with an umbrella in his hand. Daveed wondered where he spent his whole day, from where he gets his money for his food and drinks, or what he does the whole time. He returned home at night fall, his dress still neat, but you could smell toddy in his breath. His mother served him *kanji* (rice gruel) and *cherupayar* (green grams) along with fried *pappadams* (small fryums made with gram flour), after which he went to sleep in his room. He didn't know that this meal was the only one cooked in that house that day. His wife and kids wait for him to finish to have their supper. A portion of that is kept aside for breakfast the next day.

The kids eat the leftover food in the morning and go to school. In the afternoons they satisfy their hunger by drinking water from the tap. In the evening they run back home, climb the guava, mango, or some other trees to see if there are any ripe fruits to help them wait till their supper time. Though they need not pay any fees in the government-run school, Kochu Daveed decided that it was time to stop studying and look for some work. He had five good friends at school, all as poor as himself and four from the local fishermen colony. One was his neighbour and best friend, Pappu. Pappu had no father and his mother eked out a living by selling animal-shaped biscuits which she sold in her small shop along with some candies and nuts. Pappu used to share these eatables with his friends, especially Kochu Daveed, whenever he could lay hands on them when his mother was not looking. Every day after school they used to go to the seashore and sit and discuss what they would like to do in their life. It was during one of these discussions that they all decided to stop studying and learn some skill which can help them find a job. His friends decided that they would follow their fathers and become fishermen. But for Kochu Daveed they decided that he should go and learn to weld in some local workshop.

When he came home that day, he told his mother about his decision. Mariamma's eyes filled with tears. He was just fourteen years at that time and yet, she understood that her son had a maturity far beyond his age. During supper, she told her son's decision to her husband Pathro. He did not say anything in reply but just nodded his head in agreement. But in the morning before he went out he said, "Tell him to go and meet Kuttappan Asan (Master). He is my friend and he is the owner of a welding workshop." So, that day itself, Mariamma took Kochu Daveed to meet Kuttappan Asan who gladly accepted him in his workshop, but he put forward certain conditions. Inside the workshop, he is the Master and complete obedience is expected. He will be treated the same way as he treats his other workers. He will not be shown any special treatment because he is the son of his friend. He should be willing to do any kind of work and one important condition was that he should attend daily mass before he comes to the workshop. They both accepted all his conditions and decided to report for duty the next day, after early morning mass.

Attending mass early in the morning was not a very hard thing to do for Kochu Daveed. Theirs was a staunch Catholic family; they said their daily rosary without fail before supper. From a very young age, he was always asking questions to his mother about their plight, which despite praying daily, never improved. Daveed wondered, "Is God really hearing their prayers?" He always asked God for enough food for his family, but for the last one year, there was not much change in his family's situation. His mother always replied that God is listening to his prayers but is waiting to see how he would find a way to solve his problems. So, he thought that the idea that popped into his mind about going and learning a skill must be God's way of guiding him to a better life. Even then he still couldn't understand why there should be poverty in the land if God was willing to hear all the prayers and show them the way. His mother explained that the Bible gives us lots of examples of good men being tested by God with great difficulties, which they overcome and, in the end, get all the blessings from God. He did think that it was cool, but still was doubtful about why the all-knowing God should go to all these troubles just to check if the man is God-fearing or not. But he did not tell that to his mother.

Chapter 2

This is the new beginning for Kochu Daveed. He woke up early in the morning, got dressed and went to the nearby church to attend mass. He returned home, had his breakfast of old kanji and went to Kuttappan Asan's workshop. He was the first one to reach there and the gate was not yet open. He waited there till Kuttappan Asan came to open the door. He was glad to see Kochu Daveed waiting for him to open the doors. Once they entered, he went and lighted a candle in front of the framed pictures of the Sacred Heart of Jesus and the Holy Family. Other workers reached there by that time. He was introduced to everyone and then told to put on some work clothes. His mother had packed him an old pair of shirt and trousers. He went and changed into his work clothes and started his work. He was instructed to be with the lead welder, help him by handing over his tools and do the cleaning.

Time flew very fast and it was soon lunchtime. Kuttappan Asan asked him if he had brought any lunch. He replied that he would go home and have something. Asan then said, "Today you can go home for lunch, but from tomorrow you should bring something here and a cup of tea will be provided to all in the evening." He agreed, went home, told his mother what happened, had some guavas his mother had kept for him and returned to work. In the evening he was given tea and banana fry from the nearby tea shop. The work was over by 5.00 in the evening and he stayed back a little to clean the floor of the workshop. Though he was tired, he was very happy that he started well on his first day.

He returned home in a happy mood, took a shower and made himself clean. He went to his mother and started telling her about his first day at the workshop. His mother was cooking their regular supper and for the first time in his lifetime, he got his share before his father came home. By the time he finished his kanji he was feeling sleepy and after washing his hands and face he went to sleep early. He slept so well that his mother woke him up at 5.00 in the morning to get ready to go to church. This became his routine every day.

There were six people in the workshop, including him and Kuttappan Asan. Then there was the lead welder whom everyone called Maesthry and three others who did different jobs. Being the new member and the youngest in the group he was the one running here and there, doing all kinds of errands for them. In those days it was the normal practice that if one wanted to learn any kind of trade one joins a group as an apprentice, run errands for them and slowly learn the trade step by step. It would take at least three to four years' for anyone to be able to independently handle any work. Kochu Daveed decided that he was going to work hard and one day he himself will be called a Maesthry.

Around that time, Kerala government made primary education free for all. In many financially backward areas, they even had programs for serving lunch for students so that parents are encouraged to send their kids to school. But even then, kids dropped out of school by the time they were in grade eight and started to earn money for themselves. Boys normally preferred learning carpentry, masonry, welding works etc. while girls preferred to learn embroidery, stitching etc. Instead of going to proper schools to learn these trades, they preferred to join a group of people working that trade in real-life situations. Thus, they get first-hand experience in what they learn and get practical hands-on training. But first, they are made to do all kinds of odd jobs just to make them acclimatized to the field they are in.

Kochu Daveed also went through the same process. Initially, it was just cleaning the place and handing over the tools to others. Gradually he started to hold on to one end while others are welding the other end and they allowed him to open and close the gas cylinders and clean the welding rods etc. When there was a lull in the work Kuttappan Asan or the Maesthry would narrate some of their old stories where they had done some extraordinary feats of welding wonders. Kochu Daveed would sit and listen to all these tales in awe and would dream about it in the night.

While the daily routine in the workshop was training him to be a future welder, his daily routine of early morning mass has started to develop him spiritually also. The parish priest, Fr. Nelson, started to take note of this youngster attending mass daily and one day asked him whose son he was. He was surprised to know that he was the offspring of that prodigal son, Kavungal Pathro. He took a liking to this youngster who was determined to make a worthy life, unlike his father. He made a point to spend at least five minutes with Kochu Daveed after mass, giving him good advice. The youngster too started liking this old priest and waited for him daily to talk to him. He was yearning for a father figure to guide him because he felt that his own father was living in the same house but was so distanced from him.

There was one advice that Fr. Nelson gave him which he tried to follow daily. He was told to pray the rosary daily before going to bed and to read any book daily at least for ten minutes. Praying the rosary daily was easy because his mother and sisters pray that without fail every day before supper. He started to join them in their prayers. The only book that he could find in his house was the Holy Bible. So, he started reading it daily. When he told the priest that he was reading from the Holy Bible daily, the father asked him what he understood from the reading. This made him absorb what he was reading and as well as think about it. Fr. Nelson began to give him books about saints and their lives and many other books related to the mysteries of the Holy Bible.

Soon Fr. Nelson understood that Kochu Daveed was not going to be a blind follower of the faith but wanted clear answers for his doubts. He would not rest until he found a satisfactory answer to the questions that arose in his mind. Sometimes it would seem to the priest that he had awakened a sleeping giant in Kochu Daveed. Then he would question himself whether he did the right thing in encouraging reading habit in him. Instead of accepting what was written as Word of God, Kochu Daveed was comparing what was written to what was being followed by the church. His first doubt was about the statues of Mother Mary and other saints kept in the church. He wondered why we should pray to others when God clearly says, "Worship no God but me. Do not make for yourselves images of anything in heaven or on earth. Do not bow down to any idol or worship it, because I am the Lord your God and I tolerate no rivals." Although Fr. Nelson thought that Daveed was going the Protestant way, he did not express that openly. He smiled as if he was expecting this question. He explained calmly, "What you said is true. We should worship only the true God. In the Catholic church, we do not worship Mother Mary or other saints. We only ask them to intercede for us. We believe that they are the people close to God, so God would listen to them if they ask something for us. It is the same as we do in our family, we send our petitions to our father through our mother thinking that it has a better chance of being accepted."

While reading Genesis, Daveed had a doubt which he shared with Fr. Nelson: Cain killed Abel because of jealousy, which means we are all descendants of Cain, the evil one. So that must be the reason the world has so many evil people in it. The father was then expecting the question of how the world was populated if there were only three people remaining after Abel's death. He was wondering how he would handle that question. But luckily that was not asked, and Father sighed in relief. Kochu Daveed did think of asking that question but felt it would just be embarrassing for both.

There were several such questions that he asked Fr. Nelson, and only because of his age and experience, and position of trust was he able to wriggle out of some tight spots. Though he had managed to give some satisfactory answers, he knew that Daveed would come back to the same questions later. Other times he was happy that he had awakened the quest for knowledge in the youngster and he knew that he would not stray away from the path of righteousness.

Three years passed since Kochu Daveed started his apprenticeship in the workshop and his spiritual awakening in the church. It was time for the old priest Fr. Nelson to move to the Bishop's house for his last posting. Kochu Daveed was sad to see his good friend and advisor be transferred. He did not like the young priest who replaced Fr. Nelson. He thought that the young priest was enjoying himself talking and laughing with the young women in the parish and he felt that he wouldn't be able to continue the discussions with him.

At the workshop, although he had started to handle some work independently, his pay was not enough to have a good life. The good thing was that he could support his family and keep them out of starvation. Even if it was kanji they were able to have it three times daily. The thing that was worrying him now was his elder sister's marriage. She too stopped studying when she was in grade eight and started helping her mother in household work. She was beautiful like her mother and hence had several marriage proposals coming in from good families. But Pathro knew that he could not afford to have a big wedding ceremony and all he could give her was some land as a dowry.

One day, Pathro's friend Chandy came to their house with his wife. They lived about ten minutes away from their home, in Odatha. Odatha has some historical significance. The word was derived from the Dutch word *Hortha* which means garden. In the 17th century, when the Dutch were ruling Kochi, they established a botanical garden in this area, probably the first botanical garden in India. The then Dutch Governor Hendrick Van Rheede wanted to document the plant species in Kerala and this garden was a part of that mission. A book in twelve volumes called *Hortus Malabaricus* (Garden of Malabar) was published at that time. Kerala was known as Malabar at that time. Chandy and his wife came there with a marriage proposal for his youngest brother who was in the army. They brought a photograph of his brother in army uniform. He looked dashing. The only problem was that he was 10 years her senior. But that was overlooked when they said that they needed only a plot of land as dowry and that they would take care of all the wedding expenses. It was like a dream come true for Pathro. For his daughter, Annamma, it was a way to escape from the poverty in their house. Moreover, they were from a good family and the guy was handsome, although darker in complexion than her.

Even though the groom's family took care of the wedding expenses, Pathro had to sell a small plot of land to buy new clothes for the bride and others in the family. Kochu Daveed asked for a week's vacation from his workshop and ran around helping his father in the arrangements for the wedding. The groom had come a week before the marriage and visited the bride's house. Kochu Daveed liked the way his would-be brother-in-law carried himself. He looked like he was a ranked officer in the army. When he got a chance, he asked him about his rank in the army. He got the reply that he was an Hawildar (a non-commissioned officer) in the army now. But he was studying more to become a commissioned officer soon. He was very proud of his new brother-in-law, Simon. When Simon asked Kochu Daveed about his work and studies, he was embarrassed when explaining his educational background, but made sure to tell him that he likes to read a lot. Simon then suggested him to visit the corporation library in Chullickal to get a membership and start reading different books.

The wedding was a good occasion to meet all the family members and all the brothers of Pathro came with their family and made it a great celebration. Everyone helped him with cash and kind for the wedding. Kochu Daveed was really thrilled that all his rich cousins behaved naturally with him without any inhibitions. He was the shy one most of the time. Everything went as planned and the bride left with the groom the next day amidst a sea of tears from the mother and sisters.

Chapter 3

After the wedding, his sister and brother-in-law stayed only a week in Kochi. They left for Secunderabad, where he was stationed. His mother used to get letters from her regularly, detailing her life as an army man's wife. They were all happy for her. While everything was going well for his sister, trouble was brewing up in his home front. Chandy, the brother of his brother-in-law became a frequent visitor to his house. Initially everyone thought that he was visiting just to give company to his lonely father. They both would sit and talk for long hours in the evening and no one would bother them. This would happen at least three times a week and later became a daily event.

One day, Kochu Daveed's mother told him when he returned from work that they both had been drinking alcohol, that too the cheap variety, daily and that was brought home by Chandy. He was so mad on hearing that that he decided to talk to Chandy. That day while Chandy was getting ready to return home, he called him and said, "Chandy Achaya! (Achayan=Elder brother) You shouldn't let father drink too much. We thought he had reduced his consumption, but now it has become worse than before." Chandy gave a stunned look, but before he could give a reply, Pathro, his father jumped up like a lion and shouted, "You have no right to advise Chandy here. He is here because I invited him, and he is the brother of my son-in-law. He has every right to come here any time and do what he wants. You shut your bloody mouth and go back to your cheap welding job. Don't come and advise genteel people like us."

Kochu Daveed was so embarrassed at his father's words that he hung his head in shame and went back to his room. From that day onwards, he decided that he would not talk to his father anymore unless he is given some respect in the house. He also decided that one day he would leave the house and return only when he has a respectable job. His daily routine changed a little:

after he returns home from work, he took a shower, had his supper and left home immediately to the Corporation Library. There he spent his evening among books and returned home only when the library closed for the day.

He read whatever he could get his hands on. Though he liked to read novels and short stories, whenever he came across any book dealing with religion, he started to read them too. He was on a self-discovery journey. He still was a regular church goer and attended mass daily, but something was bothering him. When he started getting to know about other groups in Christianity, he felt that each group had something right in what they were saying. But he did not feel comfortable enough to go and join them. He felt that though they all talked more about finding the true Christ, their rules and regulations made them more rigid than the Catholic Church. All these Christian denominations had one thing in common, and that was their belief in Jesus Christ. But each believed that they were following the right Christ and all others were wrong. The more he read the more he came to understand that it is not the differing views of beliefs that kept these groups apart. No one was willing to sacrifice the power and control they had over their followers. Once you tasted the heady wine of power, no one was willing to relinquish it. It is true that "power corrupts, and absolute power corrupts absolutely."

A month passed since he had a showdown with his father, and nothing had come back to normal yet. He learnt from his mother that Chandy now came to the house only when he knew that Kochu Daveed was not at home. He started a new habit of bringing some food items like beef fry or shrimp fry along with the liquor. From the way his mother was talking about it he understood that everyone else in the house liked his visit, though for different reasons. His father liked the liquor and his mother and sisters liked the food he shared with them. He wanted to warn them that this was going to end in a bad way and his family was going to suffer. But he also had the feeling that no one was going to listen to him. Still, he did talk to his mother about it and shared his feelings about the safety of his family. His mother assured him that she would take care of the sisters and see to it that no harm comes to them.

He kept thinking of moving out of his house and going to some far away place and starting a new life. He had heard stories in his neighbourhood of people leaving for some big cities like Delhi and Bombay and making it big there. He had heard that one of his third cousins, Varghese, was living a good life in Bombay. He wanted to go there and try out his luck. He started asking about the whereabouts of Varghese and came to know that he lived in the suburbs of Bombay in a town called Ambernath. He managed to get the postal address of Varghese and saved that in his small diary. He thought that would help him someday.

One Sunday he decided to go and meet his old friend, Fr. Nelson, in the Bishop's house. He went there in the evening and took permission to meet him. Father Nelson was happy to see Kochu Daveed after a long time. He saw that though he looked slim, he was looking fit because of his hard work in the Bishop house. They exchanged pleasantries and then Kochu Daveed shared his thoughts of going to some big city and make a better living. Fr. Nelson thought that it was a good idea. He said that he is an adult now and he must make his own decisions. But wherever he was going, he should take care not to fall into wrong company and lose his vision of a good life. He also shared the knowledge he was gaining on different aspects of Christianity and how he sometimes has so many doubts. Fr. Nelson reassured him that it is quite common to have doubts when you read a lot. But the important thing is to remember that everyone has their own opinion on all matters, and their opinion is right for each one of them. You may not agree with their opinion but that does not mean that either of you are wrong.

Fr. Nelson also said, "My son, having the urge to know more is a sign of healthy mind. When I was young, I thought that I was right in my beliefs. But as you age you come to understand that your knowledge is not complete. There are lots of things which are beyond your understanding. Maybe, if I had decided to go, explore and widen my frontiers, I would have become someone else. But I decided to entrap myself into a rigid system which does not allow to explore beyond its boundaries. I got so busy in digging deep into the system that I forgot that there is a far greater world outside with all its splendour and now I don't have the strength to break out of this world. But you are not fettered by any chains. Break free and go explore the world. Read whatever you can. Do not limit yourself with any specific ideology. Keep in mind that there are always different ways to solve a problem. There are always different routes to reach a destination. I will pray for you always. Keep in touch with me wherever you are and whenever you have time."

After his meeting with Fr. Nelson, his mind started to look out for different options for leaving his home. He wanted to plan well what he wanted to do. But there were many variables in his plan. The only constant in his life was his desire to leave. Money, language and his attachment to his mother and sisters were the things that made him hesitate to leave his house. He decided to give a hint to his mother about his turmoil. One day during supper, he told her, "Amma, I think it is time for me to look for another job. I have learnt whatever I can from the workshop. Even though I do all the work now, I don't think I am paid enough. Do you think it is a good idea to look out for work in some other place?" His mother thought it was a good idea. She asked him, "Where would you like to go to work? Do you know any big workshops here? But whatever you do, don't go with any competitor of Kuttappan Asan." He replied, "I think I will go and try in Brunton boatyard. I hear they pay well there." His mother then replied, "Why don't you ask the help of Kuttappan Asan? He may be having some connections there." He thought that it was a good idea. He thanked his mother and went to sleep.

Next day after the day's work was over, he stayed behind and when everyone else left, he went and talked to his Asan. He began, "Asane! Do you think I can get a job in Brunton boatyard? I know that some of your former students are working there." Asan looked at him for some time and then replied," You are still too young to work there. But I know you have learnt all that I can teach you. And I know that a better pay will help you and your family. Do one thing. Go and meet Boiler Peter. I was his Asan too. He will help you. Tell him that I sent you." Kochu Daveed was so happy that instead of going home he went straight to find out Boiler Peter's house. There he met Boiler Peter, passed on the message of Kuttappan Asan and returned home only after he got an assurance that he will get a response within two days. When he reached home, he shared his excitement with his mother and admired the way she helped him in finding a way to get out of the workshop without leaving any bad feeling.

He waited impatiently for two days to be over and on the third evening he was there in front of Boiler Peter's house. On reaching there he asked, "Peter Cheta, is there any good news?" Peter smiled and said, "Yes, there is. How can I not help one of Kuttappan Asan's disciple? I talked to the manager and he agreed to take you as a paid trainee. Initially you won't be earning much, but still, it would be better than what you earn in the workshop. After a training of one year, they will make you a permanent employee, if they think you are good. If you agree to that you can come and join next Monday." He was so happy that he wanted to give Peter a hug. He thanked him so much and ran home to share the news with his mother.

The next day evening, his mother cooked some rice pudding in milk, with some sugar, cashews, and a sprinkle of cardamom powder. When Kochu Daveed came back from the workshop, she told him to get ready, and both of them went together to St. John Pattom Chapel, taking a container of the cooked rice pudding with them. They kept the container near the crucifix in the chapel, prayed for some time and then rang a small bell hanging near the window of the chapel. On hearing the bell ringing, the children playing nearby came running and gathered in front of the chapel. His mother opened the container and distributed spoonfuls of the milk rice pudding into the eager hands of the children. Some adults living nearby also came and shared the offering. When an old lady asked the reason for the offering, his mother replied, "My son got a good job in Brunton boatyard. I had prayed to our Lord that when he gets a good job, I would come and offer milk rice pudding here." When the container was empty, they went back home. They had the same rice pudding during supper and when Pathro asked his wife why she made this milk rice pudding that day, she told him about their son's new job. Pathro didn't say anything. But his wife could feel that he was happy on hearing the news, however he was not ready to acknowledge the same. She told her son what she felt, but Kochu Daveed just smiled. He was already in a happy mood; his father's reaction did not bother him. He was more determined to show his father that he is a winner.

On Sunday, after mass, he went and shared the good news with his mentor, Fr. Nelson. They sat in the garden and talked for some time. Since the boatyard was not very far from the Bishop's house, Fr. Nelson told him to come and meet him at least once a week. Kochu Daveed agreed to that. From that Monday onwards, he started his training in the Brunton boatyard. He was always willing to work hard and was a good student. Soon he was one of the very active and favorite trainees in the place. His daily routine was still the same. He did not change his habits. He started saving a little money in a small biscuit tin and hid it under his clothes in his room. He gave his mother a little more money now, but his mother maintained the same level of expenses in the house. The only additional spending was that they bought a little more meat on Sundays, which was more than enough for all of them to eat. His sister borrowed some money from him and bought some chickens. He along with his sisters built them a small cage where they came to roost in the evening. During daytime they were running around the backyard of their house. One of the sisters or his mother always kept an eye on the chickens lest some wily crow or eagle snatch them and fly away.

Although his life was slowly getting better, his father Pathro continued his old ways. There seemed to be no turning back for him. His drinking party with Chandy was still going on. His family did not interfere in that. They had left him to his own ways. Things became uncomfortable when his sister and brother-in-law visited them during their vacations. Then everyone had to show them a semblance of a family gathering, and they all had at least one lunch and supper together. Chandy was a disturbing presence in all the gatherings. Kochu Daveed made sure that he attended all the gatherings but slipped out by the time everyone started to sit around for after-lunch conversation. He also took care not to have any conversation with Chandy and they both avoided each other.

It was during this time that his sister got pregnant and as per custom, she came home for her first childbirth. Although he liked the whole family being together again, the fact that he had to deal with his sister's in-laws almost daily was not a pleasant occasion for him. As per the custom the girl returns to her mother's home when she is seven months pregnant. Her parents go to her in-law's home with seven types of sweets and with their permission bring her home. On the ninth month, it is the turn of the in-laws to visit their bride with sweets. If this was only the case, Kochu Daveed would have been very happy. But Chandy still being a regular visitor, he could not avoid meeting him because of his sister's presence. Though he tried telling his sister about his dislike, she in turn took sides with his father and thought that he was making a mountain out of a mole hill. Not only that, she became more demanding in making him show some respect to Chandy. She made him run errands when they both started drinking; making him go buy some food items to go along with the drink. Since she had the money, she made him buy beef fry, chicken fry and other delicacies from the nearby teashop. Life started to become stressful because of his sister and he just waited for her to go back, once everything was over.

Chapter 4

The birth of a child is a joyous occasion in any family. Regardless of the gender, any child is welcomed whole heartedly into the family by the parents. But the gender becomes a prickly subject for the grandparents in the husband's side. The parents of the wife are happy when their daughter gives birth to a boy or a girl, but the parents of the husband think that they were let down by their son if the first born was a girl. They think that only a son can carry on the family's name to the next generation. The girl is normally married off to another family and so she can't be the heir to the family name. Luckily here Simon didn't have any parents, so everyone was happy even though their first born was a daughter. As the only uncle of the new-born child, Kochu Daveed was happy. He bought whatever he could for the child until the mother and child left for Secunderabad after the baptism.

Once they left, the house was back to its old routine. He felt that all the happiness had left the house. Though he was relieved that he need not be civil to Chandy anymore, he missed the laughter and happy noises of the family when a baby was at home. The house became silent once more. He started to think about leaving the house again. But each time he started to think about leaving, his mother's face flashed before him. He couldn't leave her just when she had started to look forward to a peaceful life. There are still two more sisters to take care of. He began to doubt if he was just making the family as an excuse to cover up his fear of going to a strange place. He was in a dilemma. It was during that time that he came across "The Prophet" by Khalil Gibran. He was totally fascinated by it. He felt the poems in his heart. He was totally taken in by the beauty of the verses. When he read the part where a woman asks the prophet to "speak to us of children," he got so excited that he borrowed a piece of paper and a pencil and wrote it down to show it to his mother that night.

When his mother read that she grew a little sad. She understood his longing to set out on his own in his life's journey. She asked him, "My dear son, do you feel that your love towards your family is stopping you from growing wings and flying towards your future?" He replied, "Amma! I would like to go out and find out if I can create a better lifestyle for all of us. But I am not able to leave you all here without any means of income to the family." She replied, "Don't worry about us. We did survive before you started working. God will take care of us." Then she continued, "Be prepared to face any kind of difficulties. Always believe that God is with you and our prayers are always there for you. But wherever you go, be true to yourself and your God. Keep yourself pure at heart and say our Lord's prayer, which will keep you away from temptations. Do not miss your daily rosary and attend the mass whenever you can. The Satan will not touch you." Though he had started to have doubts about Satan, he did not argue with her. He had concluded that every human being has both good and evil inside them. But they don't want to take responsibility for their evil actions. So, they created a being which can be blamed for all the evil things they do. With these thoughts he went to sleep, still not decided on how to go forward with his plans for the future. That night while praying he asked God to show him a way out of this confusion.

Daveed's prayers were answered the next day. When he returned home after his work, he saw that Chandy was still there with Pathro and both were more intoxicated than normal. He was so angry on seeing this that he decided to put an end to it by any means. He walked over towards them and his father noticed that his son was coming to chastise them. So, before Kochu Daveed could open his mouth, Pathro started shouting profanities at him and threw the plates and cups at him. The profanities were such that no father could ever call a son so. This stopped the son on his tracks, and he returned to his room with tears welling in his eyes. He could see that his mother and sisters were standing in the corner of the kitchen with frightened expressions on their faces. He took a small clothes bag, filled it up with his meagre collection of dresses, took out the small tin in which he saved the money, gave some to his mother, hugged her and his sisters and walked out of the house. His mother wanted to call him back but decided against it. She understood that if she tried to stop him, he wouldn't stop, and that action might infuriate Pathro more. She said a silent prayer and asked God to protect him always.

He walked as fast as he could. He was so angry that all his emotions came out as tears in his eyes. At first, he had no idea where he was going. It was starting to get dark and luckily not many people were there outside to ask him anything. The few who saw him walking fast towards the bus stop didn't ask him anything because of his serious countenance. Once he reached the Veli bus stop, he stopped. He saw the small chapel of St. Jacob near the bus stop. He went inside and sat in one corner and started praying for guidance. There was no one except for an old lady sitting on the stairs outside, selling candles for people who would like to light some in front of the statue while praying for the intercession of the saint. Though he wanted to pray for guidance, he couldn't think of anything for some time. His mind kept replaying the scene with his father and tears kept flowing from his eyes. He calmed down a little after some time, went out and bought a pack of candles, went to the front of the chapel and lighted the candles in front of the saint's statue, came back and sat down in the corner again.

Then he started praying, "O! Yacob sleeha, please pray for me to our Lord, our God! I am leaving my home, my mother and my sisters under your protection. Protect them against all dangers. Please intercede on my behalf to our Lord, Jesus Christ. Please help my father to overcome his addiction. Let there be peace in our household. I am now leaving the comfort of my home to some unknown, distant place. Please guide my steps so that I may find the right path to a better life. Please protect me also from all dangers I may face during my journey. I submit my prayers to you so that you may intercede on my behalf to our Lord Jesus Christ."

He felt at peace with himself after he said the prayer. He wiped his tears away with the sleeve of his shirt and came out. He decided that he will travel towards India's business capital, the big city of Bombay. He didn't know whether there were trains towards Bombay currently. He first thought he would go to the Cochin Harbour Terminus Station in Wellingdon Island, which is the nearest railway station, but then decided against it because that station was the starting point for some trains, but trains coming from other parts of Kerala do not pass through. So, he got into the bus towards Ernakulam Town railway station, where he could get trains coming from the southern part of Kerala too. He reached the station and went to the Enquiry counter to check whether there are any trains towards Bombay. The guy manning the counter told him that Jayanthi Janatha Express is running behind schedule and it should reach there in half an hour. There was a board nearby with the fares to different stations written down neatly. He went and found out the fare to Bombay. He was aghast, it is too much to spend. He had heard that people need to buy a platform ticket to get inside the railway station and it costs only 50 paise. He bought one platform ticket and went inside. On enquiry he found out that there is one unreserved compartment at the end of the train and one directly behind the engine. He went and stood at the end of the long platform to get into the last compartment. Then he heard the train entering the station and he wondered if it was the sound of the train or his heartbeat that was louder. There were so many people rushing towards the doors of the compartment, he didn't have time to think. He too became a part of the crowd rushing in and got inside after some struggle. Good that he had only a small bag to carry.

He could find no seats inside and within five minutes the train left the station with a loud honk. He thought that he was lucky that he got inside the train. People started sitting wherever they could, and he also sat on the floor beside the door. He saw that people had already started dozing even in their uncomfortable sitting positions. But he was not able to relax. Though he had decided to travel without proper tickets, he was worried about being caught by the train ticket examiner. So, he asked the guy sitting next to him, "Cheta! Do you think the TTE will come to check the tickets now? I didn't get time to buy one." He replied, "Don't worry, I also didn't buy a ticket. The TTE will be checking the reserved compartments now. Only the newly appointed TTEs come and check here. You can see the huge number of people in this compartment. Even if someone comes to check, the maximum he will do is to let you off the next station, if you don't have any money. By the time the train starts you can always get back into the other unreserved compartment in the front." He was a little relieved on hearing this. After this conversation the other guy went back to sleep.

Kochu Daveed could not sleep. His mind kept replaying all the scenes from the evening. He then remembered that he had prayed only to Yacob sleeha, he should be praying directly to Lord Jesus Christ and ask for the intersession from his Holy Mother Mary. So, sitting there he went through one full rosary and said whatever prayers he could remember. After this exercise his mind was somewhat calm. The long tiring day and the rhythmic movement of the train so made him sleepy and he was soon fast asleep, leaning on the guy sitting near him. He woke up with a start when he heard some commotion. He opened his eyes and saw that it was already early morning and the train had

stopped in some big station. He could hear the vendors crying out and selling tea, coffee, breakfast items like idly, vada, sambar etc. He could see that there were some new faces in the compartment. He was feeling hungry as he had not eaten anything since yesterday afternoon. So, he got up, washed his face in the sink, told the guy sitting next to him to keep an eye on his seat, stepped out into the station and bought a cup of tea and a packet of Glucose biscuits because they were cheap. He decided to restrict his spending as much as he could, so that he should not be starving until he finds a good job.

The train still has 24 hours to reach Bombay. Still one full day and night to go. He didn't know how he would survive this journey. He decided that he would try and get a proper seat at least by night. Though the day was hot, since both the doors of the train were open, he could feel the wind, which did help in cooling down. His thoughts kept returning to his family, and each time he would start praying for them. He thought that it was an irony that when he had his family near him, he was trying to find faults in his religion and now when he is alone, he has started praying to all the saints he could remember.

He was feeling restless the whole day. By afternoon he was able get a proper seat. Luckily there was no visit by the ticket examiner. Gradually his thoughts started to move away from his family and began to go towards his near future. What was he going to do once he reached Bombay? He had his cousin's address with him. But he didn't want to go there unannounced. The pride in him did not want to go begging immediately on arriving his destination. He decided that it was of no use to get worried now. He did not know what the future had in store for him. But he believed in God and thought that whoever made him decide to leave the house will also take care of him. He was ready to face the challenges. Whenever he felt that he had taken a rash decision, the face of his father and Chandy appeared in his mind, which was more than enough to strengthen his mind against all challenges.

When the main lights were turned off for the night, he sat there and dozed off like everyone. He dreamed of so many things, which he wouldn't remember when he woke up. But most of his dreams left him all alone in a barren wasteland, with no clue of how he reached there or how he could get out of there. He woke up very early and he could see the twilight before the sunrise through the train window. He watched the sun slowly rise and, in its light, he could see that he was somewhere in the suburbs of Bombay. The train passed many small stations and each one had a slum area attached to it. People were going around with their daily chores, outside their small huts made of an assortment of things like tin sheets, plastic sheets, tarpaulin, mud bricks, and so on. A thought popped up suddenly into his mind; he is also going to be a part of this world. But he did not let that thought break his spirit. He said to himself that God is with him and he will come out of this as a winner.

By mid-morning the train entered a large station. He could read the name Victoria Terminus and he understood that he had reached his destination. He got down slowly onto the platform and felt the first touch of foreign soil far away from his home. He didn't know whether to be happy or sad. He closed his eyes for a minute and said the Lord's prayer. Then he went to one side away from the rush and sat on a bench made of cement to decide on what to do next.

Chapter 5

After the first euphoria of reaching the destination, Kochu Daveed began to plan his day. First things first, he wanted to freshen up first. He had heard that there would be bathrooms in the railway stations where you can get a shower for a fee. So, he went in search of it and found it near the exit. He paid 25 paise and freshened himself. Once he came out, he went to the tea stall and had tea and a small bun. The guy serving tea looked like he was from his place. So he spoke to that guy in Malayalam (the language of his place) and asked him, "Cheta, could you please tell me the name of the area where I can find work as a welder?" The guy smiled and said, "You must be new to the place. You won't get any welding jobs in the city. For that you must go to the suburbs where there are industrial estates. Try Thane, Bhayender or Andheri areas." Saying that he continued serving other customers. While coming out after finishing his tea, he heard that guy shouting at him, "The trains for the suburbs are on the other side. And don't forget to buy a ticket. They are very strict here." He said thanks and walked to the other side of the station, wondering all the while, why did that guy tell me to buy tickets? How did he know that I travelled this far without tickets? He was confused but kept walking.

He found the ticket counter for suburban trains and there was a long queue in front of it. While waiting there he debated whether to go and find the whereabouts of his cousin, Varghese, but then decided against it. "Let me try to find a job on my own first. Then I can go to his house. He should be there as a back up only." When his turn came, he bought a return ticket for Thane and back. Though it was mid-day, the train was still full of people. When he got down at Thane station, he enquired about the industrial area. He had to take a bus from there to reach it. He got down at the beginning of the industrial area and started walking. He could see that most of the big units have big walls and the gates closed. He could hear the clatter of metals and some sounds indicating grinding and cutting of metals. He thought that at least he had come to the right place on the first day itself. God must be keeping an eye on him, he thought. Though he walked the whole length of the first street, he did not have the courage to go and knock on any gates.

The sun was beating down mercilessly and he knew that he had to take a step forward and knock on some door. He gathered his courage and went and knocked on one of the gates. A man came out. He looked like a security guard. He asked, "Kya Chahiye? ("What do you want?" in Hindi, the local language). Though Kochu Daveed was not fluent in Hindi, he remembered some words from his school days. So he replied, "Kaam" (Work). The guard replied, "Kaam Nahi, Jao!" (No work, go away!). Crestfallen, he walked towards the next gate. There he saw a board near the gate with the words "No Entry without permission." He didn't have the courage to enter there. By the time he had covered four streets like this, he heard a loud siren from some factory and people started coming out of the workplaces. He assumed that it must be 5.00 p.m. He followed a group of people to the bus stop and reached back to Thane station. From there he wanted to board the train towards Victoria terminus, but each train was so fully packed that he could not board it. This must be the peak time, he thought. Since he had not eaten anything after his breakfast he decided to go out of the station and have tea. Anyhow, he did not have a place to go in a hurry. He decided to wait till the peak time is over. After nearly an hour he was able to board a train. He got down at Victoria Terminus and went and sat on a bench to plan his next move.

He looked around the platform where he was sitting. There were people everywhere. "I don't think they are as homeless as me. I have no place to go now. What will I do?" Though he knew that such thoughts will not comfort him, his mind was pushing him in to more such depressing thoughts. He thought about his failures of that day. He was not able to talk to anyone about job today. His belief in God started to wane. "Why didn't you help me today? Did you lead me so far from home just to abandon me?" he asked God. Tears of self-pity welled his eyes. Then he saw two policemen come there swinging their long canes and chasing away a small group of boys from the platform. They all ran past him and he saw that there were not only boys but a small woman with a child in her hand, an older guy, presumably her husband and a girl too. Looked like a whole family of ragpickers.

Suddenly he realised that his condition is not as bad as theirs. He was at least allowed to sit there in the railway station. It was getting dark and he decided to stay there in the platform for that night. He looked around and saw some train compartments parked little away from the station. He thought about walking over there to see whether the doors were open. If they were open, he could sleep inside the compartment. He slowly walked towards the end of the platform and got down onto the tracks. Keeping an eye on any incoming trains, he moved towards the empty compartments. It was quite dark now and there were no lights in that area. He walked very carefully. He didn't want to get into any tripping and falling accident. He walked along the side of the parked compartments looking for any open doors. He noticed that the doors were high up because he was standing on the ground level. He must climb four steps to enter through the door. He saw that one door was open a little. So he climbed the steps and entered the compartment. Just as he was about walk into the corridor, he saw some dark figures moving at the other end. He stopped and peered ahead. He could make out the figures of the two policemen and two smaller figures. Must be the people from the ragpickers family. Luckily, they didn't notice him yet. He quickly jumped out of the train and walked as fast as he could to the platform.

He was out of breath when he got into the safety of the platform. His heart was pounding. He thanked God for his narrow escape. He suddenly remembered that the local trains stop running by midnight and that there would be no one on this platform. He had noticed that when he was checking for the train timings in the morning. He didn't want to stay there and come face to face with those policemen again. He walked quickly and went towards the platforms from where the long-distance trains start their journey. They were on the other side of the station.

Just to be on the safe side, he purchased a platform ticket and entered it. He thought that being a part of a crowd was safer than sitting alone somewhere. There were lots of people milling around in this area and he felt safe. He found and empty spot and became one among the long-distance passengers waiting for the train.

He sat there and went through all that happened that whole day. He thought that his first day in Bombay will be remembered by him always for its mixture of excitement and disappointment. He remembered his mother and decided to pray one rosary for the blessings of that day. He was feeling quite tired and he didn't know when he fell asleep. When he woke up it was dawn again. He was lying in a foetal position in the same bench he sat the previous night. He sat up and checked if his small bag was with him. He was lying with his head on it. He felt relieved. He looked around and saw that there were different people all around him. He went and used the pay and use washroom and freshened up again, went to the same tea shop and had tea and bun. While having tea he noticed that it was Saturday. So, he decided to go in search of his cousin Varghese in Ambernath. Most probably it might be a half working day. He didn't want to go there early in the morning. So he went and checked the train timings. There was one slow train to Ambernath at 11.00 a.m. and he decided to take that. He went around the whole station to see whether there were any other places where he could spend that night also. He didn't want to be a burden to his cousin.

By the time he reached his cousin's house it was almost 2.00 in the afternoon. It was a three-storied building and his cousin's apartment was in the ground floor. This housing complex looked bigger and more spacious than the surrounding ones and he gathered that his cousin was leading a good life here. He went in and rang the bell. Someone opened the door a little and he could see that there was a chain attached to the door. Through the gap in the door he could hear a lady's voice asking who he was. He introduced himself as Kochu Daveed from Fort Kochi, son of Kavungal Pathro and cousin of Varghese. The lady did not open the door but went inside and he saw a man opening the door. It was his cousin Varghese. He was a little apprehensive about his welcome, but the beaming face of Varghese cleared all his doubts. Varghese gave him a hug and wondered aloud, "What are you doing here, Kochu Daveed?" He replied, "I came here to look for some work, Cheta." "So, where are you staying and when did you come?" he asked. "I am staying with my friend near Victoria Terminus. I came here yesterday" he replied. Then Varghese said, "I just returned from my office and was going to have my lunch. Come and have lunch with me first. Then we will talk." He agreed to it without any objection. He saw Sheela Chechi, wife of Varghese Chetan, laying out the plates on the table. She smiled at him and said, "I didn't recognise you. That's why I went and called Chetan before opening the door. We should be very careful here. This is Bombay, and many have been duped after opening the doors to strangers." He said that he understood. She served him rice, fish curry, fish fry and a vegetable dish. Tears welled in his eyes for a moment. He felt like he had not tasted proper food in ages, though it had been only less than a week. He remembered his mother again. But he was careful not to show his feelings to others. He could not eat much as his stomach must have adjusted itself to the meagre food for the last few days. After lunch they sat in the living room, and then Varghese asked him, "Did you find any work here?" He replied, "No Cheta, I was hoping you could help me find one." Varghese thought for a moment and said, "I work in a textile factory. There is not much welding work there. We have a maintenance crew that takes care of our machineries. I will check with them if they are willing to take someone as a trainee. If you had known typewriting or shorthand, I could try for an office clerical job. Keep trying in the industrial areas in north Bombay. Something should turn up. Don't lose hope."

Though he was little disappointed by this reply, he understood the situation. Then they started sharing the news about his people back in his town. By evening, they had tea and he got up to take leave. But Varghese insisted that he stay there that night, go to church the next day, as it was Sunday and then return to his friend's place after lunch. He readily agreed to the plan and stayed there that night. He had such a peaceful night after so many days and, the next day after mass and lunch he returned to Victoria Terminus, his home away from home, he thought wryly.

Sitting in a bench in the platform, he was a little happy about the outcome of his visit. He has at least someone who he could call in time of need in this big city. Sheela Chechi had packed some roti and vegetables for him and his friend. He knew he could use that till the following day. Also, he received some rarely used old shirts and pants from Varghese Chetan, which were too tight for him. They fitted him very well. From tomorrow he would start his job hunting, till that time he thought he could go out of the station and have a look around the city. He returned to the station by night, purchased a platform ticket and went back to the platform where the long-distance trains start.

The whole of the following week saw him going around different industrial areas in search of a job. He was now ready to do any kind of job, but he found no job. The money he had with him was running out. So, he decided to spend as little as he could. He drank water from the pipes on the wayside, ate peanuts for lunch most of the time, which were sold on the roadsides by old women. His breakfast and supper were mostly tea and bun. The heat from the sun was burning him down too. He lost his fair complexion and he was as dark as the kids playing in the streets. Sometimes he was so desperate that he started to wonder if there was ever a God in this world. Why would the Almighty give him so mush distress? He started doubting himself, shouted profanities to himself for being such a fool and leaving his comfortable hometown. He was angry at God, his father, who was the root cause for his leaving, his mother, who did not stop him while he was leaving home, and above all at himself for taking such a drastic step and now suffering in this God forsaken place.

By night fall he was back in Victoria terminus, with his platform ticket, taking care not to stay at the same place twice in a row. His sleep was always fitful, never a peaceful one, always having nightmares, most of the time waking up with a start from a nightmare which always ends in him running after a vanishing train, or, walking in a narrow, twisted path which always ends in a huge abyss. He did not stop his daily prayers and rosary. Prayers did help him raise back for a short time from the depths of self-pity he had fallen into. He still had a glimmer of hope that God did not guide him this far without a reason. He did wonder how long he could withstand this torturous life. He could feel that he was getting weaker.

On Friday morning, he was feeling too tired to get up from the cement bench he was sleeping. He knew the reason. He had not had a proper meal after the one he had from Varghese Chetan's house. His stomach was upset from last night and he had to use the pay and use toilet many times in the night. Though he had only little money left, he decided to have a lemon juice with salt to save himself from dehydration. He had learnt this from his mother when he used to fall sick at home. Once he had that he was feeling better. He thought he would go for the job hunt one more day and then if nothing happens, he would go and get some help from Varghese Chetan.

He went around a different industrial estate till afternoon with no success. He could not bear any more heat in his weakened condition, so when he saw a compound that looked like a park, he went towards it. Only when he reached the gate did he understand that it was a cemetery. There were lots of trees in it to give shade and there was a small chapel in the middle. The cemetery looked well maintained and he found the reason when he went inside through the open gate. All the tombs were big ones with English names engraved on them. Must be an old one from the time of British rule in India, he thought. He went and sat on one of the tombs under a huge tree. The thick canopy and the cool breeze in his face gave him a pleasant feeling and he felt quite calm. He turned around and was trying to read the name of some English General when he felt that the earth was swallowing him, and he fell into darkness.

Chapter 6

Kochu Daveed felt someone sprinkling water in his face and woke up with a start. He saw a small group of people around him. He was clueless about his whereabouts. He looked around and saw that he was sitting on a tomb in a cemetery. He suddenly remembered that he had sat on this tomb in the shade of a large tree to escape the burning sun. How long ago was that? A lady with a broom was asking him something. He could not understand her language. The lady must be speaking in Marathi, the local language. Then an old man started to speak to him slowly in Hindi. He understood that he was asking why he was sleeping here. He tried to explain in his broken Hindi that he came and sat here because the sun was too hot, and he fell asleep or became unconscious. Then the old man explained that it was morning now and he was lying there in the cemetery the whole night. The old lady who came to sweep the chapel saw him first and thought that he was a dead body. They all laughed at that. He felt a shiver going up his spine when he heard that. He wanted to get up, but he felt dizzy and sat down again. Someone brought him a soda and he drank that. He could hear his stomach rumbling. The lady with the broom and the old man must have heard it too. They helped him to walk towards the steps of the chapel and made him sit there. The old man gestured with his hands and told him to wait there and he walked towards the gate. All others except the lady with the broom left. She continued sweeping the pathway to the chapel.

He sat there and thought about what had happened until now. He remembered the stories his grandmother used to tell him about ghosts in the cemetery, which come out at midnight and drink the blood of any unsuspecting man in the vicinity of the cemetery. She used to tell him mostly to make him stay indoors at night when he was a small kid visiting their farm. He imagined how she or his mother would react if they had known that he had slept in the cemetery the whole night. He corrected himself with a small smile, he did not sleep there; he was lying there unconscious. He knew that he was not that brave enough to go there voluntarily in the night. He thought of going inside the chapel to pray, but he decided to wait for the old man, who he saw coming towards him. He had a glass of tea in one hand and a package in the other. He gave the tea to him and motioned him to drink. Then he opened the package and gave him rusks to eat with the tea. The old man sat there with him till he finished his rusks and tea. He joined his palms together and thanked the old man. The old man just smiled, patted on his shoulder and left with the empty glass.

He heard sweeping sound from inside the chapel. So, he got up and went inside. He knelt and started praying. After the prayers he went towards the woman and joined his palms to say thanks. She just held his palms and smiled. He was feeling very peaceful. He felt the touch of God in both the woman's and the old man's touch. A thought crossed his mind that this must be Mother Mary and St. Joseph, sent to help him by the Lord Jesus Christ. That image lingered in his mind for a long time till he reached Victoria Terminus. He decided to go and meet Varghese Chetan after freshening up at the station. He thought to himself, it was Saturday, so Varghese Chetan will be home in the afternoon. He thought it is better to go in the evening, so as not to disturb their lunch time.

He reached Ambernath by 4.00 in the evening and he was surprised to find that Varghese Chetan and family were genuinely happy on seeing him. After tea and biscuits, he informed them that he was planning to leave Bombay as he has not found any job yet. Then Varghese asked him, "Where are you planning to go?" He replied, "I have no idea." "Why don't you try in Visakhapatnam, I hear that they are doing lots of work in the new shipyard?" Varghese asked. He thought that it was a good idea. Shipyard means lots of welding works. He was hopeful that he would find some job there. Varghese then continued, "There will be lots of contractors doing piece works for the shipyard, try with them first. You might get a chance." He was wondering if he would like to risk one more ticketless travel, when Varghese asked him, "Do you have money for the train ticket? You may have to change at least two or three trains to reach there." Then he replied, "No Cheta, I don't think I have that much money." "Don't worry, I will help you with the ticket. I was not able to help you with a job; this is the least I can do to help you" said Varghese. He was overjoyed on hearing that. He thanked him for his generosity. Once again, he thanked God silently. He thought that God is still guiding him towards his destiny. All he had to do was to follow his guidance.

Varghese told him, "Come let's go to Kalyan station. The ticket counter closes only at 8.00 p.m. Let us see if we can get tickets for tomorrow." Luckily, they were able to book tickets for the Sunday night train. He must change three trains to reach there. But he was happy with that. As long as he had the tickets, he was ready to face any travel. Varghese insisted that he stay with them that night and leave only after mass and lunch on Sunday. He agreed to that.

Everything went as planned. He had a good night's sleep and good food on his last day in Bombay. Sheela Chechi had packed some rotis also for the journey. While leaving the house after lunch, Varghese gave him some money too. Kochu Daveed was really touched by this gesture and tears welled in his eyes. He said his farewell and went to Kalyan station. He was used to living on the platforms by now, so waiting for the train the whole afternoon and evening was not tiresome for him. He just enjoyed the freedom he felt with the ticket in his pocket. He need not be on the lookout for the train ticket examiners anymore. He had a valid ticket and he was very happy about it. He thanked God again for the way he was being guided. He could feel hope rising in his heart. While waiting for the train, he sat there and thought about the irony in his life situation. He had heard stories of how people from his place would travel to Bombay and when they return after some time, they all looked successful in life. Only when he had reached Bombay, did he understand that life is not as rosy as it seemed. He knew the life of people before they left for Bombay and after they returned from Bombay. But he had not seen how their life had transformed there or how much challenges they must have faced there to become successful.

Every one of them must have gone through the same phases as him. They must have stayed persistent in the face of difficulties and succeeded in the end.

A thought suddenly flashed in his mind, "Am I running away from challenges?" Then he consoled himself. He did survive for two weeks here in near homeless situation. He was just shown a different path and he decided to take it. Whatever be the situation he was not going to return home unless he finds a job and prove that he could stand on his own feet.

The train journey this time was more a relaxing one. He was able to sleep well in his berth. He enjoyed watching the countryside sceneries rushing past from him while the train was at full speed. He thought of his mother and sisters back home. He realized with a guilty feeling that he had not thought of them for the past few days when he was going around looking for work. He consoled himself that he was too focused on surviving that he did not think of anything else. Should he write home to his mother and inform her that he is now in Visakhapatnam, when he reached there? He then decided against it. "Let me find some work first, then I will write a long letter" he told himself. There were some hours of waiting time in each main junction and he had to switch trains. He took all that in his stride and never once thought that this was all a futile exercise. He kept his hopes alive in his heart, kept praying whenever he could and by the morning of the third day, he reached his destination, Visakhapatnam, in the state of Andhra Pradesh.

Visakhapatnam is the largest city and the financial hub of the State of Andhra Pradesh. It is the home to the oldest shipyard in India and the only natural harbour in the east coast of India. The local language is Telugu and Kochu Daveed had no idea on how to communicate in that language. But he was not really worried about that now. He had survived the last two weeks out of his hometown without knowing the local language. He knew, by the Grace of God, he would survive here also. He freshened up in the train itself as much as he could before getting down. After having a light breakfast, he managed to find out the bus route to the shipyard area. Unlike Bombay, he felt a little more at ease with himself, maybe because he was still in South India. He went around the shipyard area just to get the feel of the place. He saw the huge arch at the entrance of the shipyard. He knew that he could not go inside. He walked along the opposite side of the road and turned in to smaller streets looking for welding workshops. Suddenly a name board caught his attention. It said, "Nair's Tea shop." He stopped there in front of the tea shop. Nair is one of the common Hindu surnames in his state. So, he knew that whoever is the owner of the shop is a Malayali. He went inside and saw this older gentleman in white dhoti and shirt, seated at the cash counter. He had a pleasant face with salt and pepper beard and a neat line of holy ash in his forehead. Behind him, on the wall there were small framed pictures of Lord Ayyappan and some other Hindu Gods.

He went straight to the guy and spoke to him in Malayalam, "Cheta, I am new to this place. I came here looking for work. I am a welder by profession. Do you know any place where I could find some work?" The guy smiled and asked, "What is your name, Aniya (little brother) and where do you come from?" "I am Kochu Daveed and my hometown is Kochi" he replied. The guy said, "There are many people from our state managing their own workshops and doing contract work for the shipyard. I know some of them who come here for food. But I have to talk to them and see if they need someone." He continued, "My wife and I have been running this shop for the past five years. We have seen lots of Malayalis working in this area. Our sons used to help us out here. Now both are in Hyderabad for higher studies. You look like you are the same age as my elder son. Do you think you can help us here till you find your job?" Kochu Daveed was so stunned by this sudden turn of events that he was speechless for some time. He was wondering whether he heard it right? Was this stranger helping him just like that? Then he thought, "God's way of helping will be like this, totally unexpected." Nair mistook his silence for hesitance and said, "I just gave you an option for the time being. It is okay if you don't like it."

Kochu Daveed replied immediately, "No Cheta! I was just surprised to get such an offer from you. I would gladly help you out till I find a job. I need a place to sleep at night. That's the only request I have now." On hearing this Nair said, "You need not worry about that. You can sleep here in this tea shop at night. We don't have any customers after 9.00 p.m. So, we close at that time. Our house is nearby, and we open the shop at 5.00 a.m. All you need to do is to clean up the place before you sleep and wake up when we come in the morning. You can have whatever food we cook here, but for the time being I will not be paying you anything until I see how you work. Is that good for now?" Kochu Daveed agreed to it immediately. Man's basic needs, food and shelter, are being offered for his work and he was willing to accept that. He saw God's hand in everything, and he was ready to accept whatever he was being offered. If this is the way God wants to begin his new life, then he was not going to oppose it. He would just go along with the plan of God, which he thought would always guide him through the unknown paths.

Nair offered him some old clothes of his son to wear during his work hours. Although the shop was known as the tea shop, breakfast, lunch and dinner was served as well. Nair's wife was the main cook. Nair took care of the service and bill payments. Kochu Daveed's main duty was to remove the plates after the customer had finished eating and deliver to the backyard where an old lady was washing the dishes. He must bring in the clean plates back to the shop. He was also supposed to clean the tables when the customer gets up from the chair. His duties included helping the dish-washing lady when there was too much rush in the shop, especially during lunch time.

Life started to have some routine. He wakes up around 4.30 in the morning, freshens himself up in the backyard, keeps everything ready by the time Nair and his wife came in. They all have a tea in the morning before anyone starts to come in. By 6.00 in the morning, customers begin to tickle in for breakfast and tea or coffee. Then there is a lull till 11.30, and during this time Mrs. Nair prepares lunch items. After lunch comes more teatime followed by dinner time by 7.00 in the evening. Normally there is no one by 8.00 p.m. He starts cleaning the place and when the owner couple leave the shop by 9.00 p.m. he is ready to sleep after a hard day's work. Before he goes to bed, he kneels in front of the benches he had arranged side by side, making a temporary cot and completes one full rosary. He thinks of his family before he sleeps and prays to God to protect them.

Within two weeks he begins to recognise the regular customers and starts to help Nair in serving them. Though he wanted to ask Nair about his welding job, he controlled himself by saying that everything will happen in God's own time. He concentrated on doing his job in the best way he could. Nair was happy that he found a hard-working boy to help him. After two weeks he started to give him some money as wages every Sunday. The shop did not close even on Sundays because there were labourers from other parts of the country who had nowhere else to go to get some food any cheaper than this. They were also not willing to cook on their own because that was the only day they could rest for some time. Comparatively, Sundays had less customer volume than other days, but Nair did not want to lose any kind of income. On the third Sunday, Kochu Daveed asked Nair if it was possible for him to visit the nearby church once a week. Nair immediately consented to his request and told him to take half a day off on Sundays to attend mass. He found out the church by asking around and he had to take a bus to reach there. Though the mass was conducted in Telugu, he felt happy that he could now continue going to church. It was in this church that he met Mr. Thomas who was to become his next guide towards his new life.

Chapter 7

It was more than a month since he started working in Nair's tea shop. One Sunday while he was coming out of the church after mass, he saw a gentleman in neat shirt and pants who looked like he was from Kerala. He didn't know what made him think that he was from Kerala. He just looked different. He had become a little more outgoing since he had started working in the tea shop. So, without any hesitation he went towards the gentleman and asked him in Malayalam, "Hello Cheta, are you from Kerala?" The man smiled and said, "Yes, I am from Kottayam." On hearing this Kochu Daveed said, "I knew immediately when I saw you that you are a Malayali. I am from Kochi and I work in a tea shop here." He continued, "I came here looking for some welding job, but I could got a job only at the tea shop. I am hoping to get into some mechanical work field soon."

The guy thought for some time and said. "I am a small sub-contractor in the shipyard. My name is Thomas and I will look out to see if I could find some work for you. Where can I find you if I want to see you?" Kochu Daveed said that he lives quite near to the Shipyard, in Nair's tea shop and everyone in that area knows where the shop is. He replied, "I know Nair. I used to be his customer when I first came here. I stopped going there when I moved to my new place. It is quite far from there." "Anyhow, it was nice meeting you here. I will surely inform you if there is any job openings" he continued, and they parted ways.

Kochu Daveed was happy that he met Thomas and he had a glimmer of hope that he would help him. When he returned to the shop, he told Nair about meeting Thomas. Nair also remembered Thomas and said that he is a very good man. A week went by without any developments. Everyone was well into their routine work. On Saturday evening, he was busy in the backyard helping the old lady finish her dishes, when he heard Nair calling him. He came out to the front, drying his hands in his shirt when he saw that Thomas was also there with Nair. He smiled at them and wished him a good evening in a respectful tone. Nair spoke first, "Kochu, Mr. Thomas wants to take you as a helper in his team. Are you willing to go with him?" Kochu Daveed couldn't hide his surprise and joy. With beaming face, he replied, "I am ready to do anything. But who is there to help you?" Nair said, "Don't worry about me. We will manage without you as we had done before." Then Thomas spoke, "Come to the church tomorrow morning. I will take you to my place from there if that is okay with both of you." They both agreed to that. Thomas left after having tea with them.

That night Kochu Daveed couldn't sleep properly. After Mr. and Mrs. Nair left, he sat there in the bench thinking of all the good things that had happened since he left home. He thanked God for everything, especially the way he was guiding him from one place to another, without any harm to his body or soul. Tomorrow his life is going to take a new turn. He knew and believed that God will take care of him. When the Nairs came in the morning to open the shop, they found him up and ready to go. They gave him some money and they had breakfast together. Nair said that his tea shop is always open for him if he needs anything. Kochu Daveed thanked them both with his whole heart and took leave from them. He reached the church quite early with his small bag of belongings. During mass he shed tears of gratefulness and thanks to the Lord who takes care of him. After mass he met Thomas who took him to the bus stand and caught a bus to his new home.

Thomas took him to a small tiled house with a small front yard, which opens directly to the street. There was a wall separating it from the street but no gate. In the verandah a middle-aged man was sitting in one of the cane chairs and reading the newspaper. He got up when he saw them and smiled. Thomas introduced him and said, "Ouseph Cheta, this is Kochu Daveed. You can call him Kochu. He will be your new helper." He turned around and said to Kochu, "This is Ouseph Chetan, our chief welder. He has been with me from the time I started this small company. You are going to help him and learn to do onsite welding works." Ouseph asked him, "Do you know anything about welding?" Kochu Daveed replied, "Yes Cheta, I learned it from our Kuttappan Asan in Kochi and I had worked for some time in Brunton Boatyard also." "I have heard of Kuttappan Asan. I am from Vypeen Island near Kochi. My brother-in-law used to work with him. You must be good if you had trained with him." Thomas said, "Come, let's go inside and I will introduce you to others. Everyone must be in the kitchen now, preparing for lunch." They met four guys in the kitchen. Thomas introduced them, "This is Saju from Kollam, Nizar from Malappuram, Biju from Kottayam and Reghu from Ernakulam." "This is Kochu Daveed from Kochi. He is our new member in the team. He will be helping Ouseph Chetan. Let me show your room. You will be sharing it with Ouseph Chetan. We have four rooms here. I use one room and two people each share the other rooms. There is a bathroom and toilet in the backyard, also a well from which water is drawn. There is a drinking water line from the corporation. The tap is at the back. But we get water from it only in the morning. We collect water from it for our drinking and cooking purposes."

He took him to his room while talking. There were two foldable cots made of metal and plastic in the room. One of them had a bed with the bedsheets and pillows placed neatly. The other one had a thin bed rolled and kept to one side. Thomas pointed to the rolled-up bed and said, "You can sleep in that. Another guy used to be here. He went back to Kerala because his mother was not well, and he decided to stay back there to help her. I will give you a bed sheet and pillow. Keep your things here in this room and let us go for lunch."

Everyone was there in the kitchen. Each took a plate and filled it with rice, poured some curried yogurt in to it and took a chicken piece from the saucepan in the stove. They came to the small room in the centre of the house which served as the dining room and living room. There was only a small writing table in one corner with two chairs beside it. Thomas and Ouseph sat on them. The others sat on the metallic folding chairs lying around the room and holding the plate in their hands started eating.

While chatting around and having his lunch, Kochu Daveed got to know more about the household practices. Only on Sundays they do the cooking here. In the morning they normally have plain bread and tea. Only Thomas goes to church on Sundays. The others stay back and cook mostly rice and chicken. They have the same thing in the night also. Other days they have an arrangement with the tea shop near their workshop, where they have their breakfast, lunch and tea. For supper they normally come home and cook some rice gruel and eat it with pickles. Everyone takes turn in cooking.

After lunch everyone went for a small nap. Kochu Daveed was not used to sleeping in the afternoon. So, he sat in the verandah and read the old Malayalam newspaper that Ouseph was reading in the morning. Everyone woke up by 5.00 in the evening and someone made black tea for everyone. They all sat together in the verandah and had it. He got to know more about the other inmates. Before supper, Thomas called him to his room and said, "I normally pay everyone a monthly salary. I have not decided on what to give you. It depends on how you work here. Do you have any questions about that? If you need some money as advance, I can give that." Kochu Daveed replied, "No Cheta, I don't need any money now. After one month give me some money which I can send it to my parents. You can keep the rest with you and give it to me when I return home. It will be safe in your hands. I might spend it foolishly if I keep it with me."

By evening he got more familiar with everyone. Before going to sleep that day, he knelt beside his cot and said his daily rosary and thanked God for showing mercy on him. Though it was a new place to him he slept very peacefully that night and woke up by 4.30 in the morning as it had become a habit now. He could hear the snoring sounds of everyone, so he lay there for some time not wanting to disturb anyone. He got up when he heard someone moving around. He went out and saw Nizar going out with a toothbrush into the backyard. He waited till he returned and saw him laying down a small mat and facing North East he started to pray his Namaz. When he was done praying, he folded his mat and asked him, "Why are you up so early? You must have not slept well because it is a new place for you." Kochu replied, "I am used to waking up at 4.30 in the tea shop. It has become a habit now." He then asked, "Do you get up so early, just to pray?" Nizar replied, "This is my Fajr prayer or the dawn prayer. We are told to pray five times daily." Kochu was amazed to hear that. All his life so far, he had been living around Christian community and he had not known about any other religions or their practices.

Nizar asked him, "Would you like to have a black tea? I am going to make some. Go brush your teeth and come. We will have it together." By the time he freshened up and returned, the black tea was ready. They both took a cup each and went and sat in the verandah. While enjoying the tea and the sunrise they shared details about their families and hometown. Slowly, one by one started to wake up and they could hear people getting ready. They all left together by 7.30, walked for about fifteen minutes and reached a small workshop. Thomas opened the door, went inside and lighted a candle in front of a small framed photo of the Holy Family and each one went to their respective pieces they were working on the previous day and started working. They were working in pairs and Thomas was overseeing each team. Kochu started helping out Ouseph and they were busy till around 9.30 when they took a break and went for their breakfast in the nearby tea shop. Thomas opened an account for Kochu there and the shop owner just wrote down the amount into a big book after they ate. Thomas explained that he will be paid by the end of the month. They continued working, taking small breaks for lunch and tea and stopped by 6.00 in the evening.

His first day went by so fast that he didn't get time to think of anything else. Everyone was impressed with the way he worked but didn't show that openly because they did not want him to feel too confident. He was tired but happy. By 8.00 in the evening everyone was relaxing after the rice gruel supper. Some went to their rooms while Kochu, Nizar, and Reghu sat in the verandah and started talking. Religion came into their topic of discussion and Kochu wanted to know more about Islam and their practices. Reghu was more inclined towards atheism and so he was not interested in the discussions anymore. He said that if he stayed there, he would have to get onto verbal duel with someone. Saying that he went to his room to sleep.

When they were alone Nizar started to explain the five pillars of Islam and the requirement that they were to pray five times daily. Kochu asked him, "I didn't get time to notice you. Did you complete your prayers while we were at work?" Nizar replied, "Yes, I did the Dhuhr (noon) and the Asr (afternoon) prayers in the workshop corner. I finished the Maghrib (sunset) prayer after coming home. The Ishaa (night) prayer I complete before going to bed." Kochu was amazed that he was so punctual in his prayer habits. Then Nizar said something that amazed him more. He said, "Did you know that the Jesus Christ and his mother Mary are mentioned in our Holy Quran?" He was totally dumbfounded. Nizar continued, "In fact Maryam, mother of Prophet Essa (Jesus) was the only woman mentioned by name in the Holy Quran, and there is one chapter dedicated to her alone." His curiosity was up when Kochu asked, "Is there a Malayalam translation of the Holy Quran? Will I be able to read it?" Nizar smiled and said, "Yes, like the Holy Bible, Holy Quran is also translated in many languages, but while praying we always use Arabic only to maintain the purity of its language." It was time for them to sleep, so they went to their respective rooms. As usual he said his daily rosary, but that day he was more in awe of Mother Mary who had a special place in other religions too.

The next few days went on like his first day. After work he helped whoever was working in the kitchen that day. His discussions with Nizar kept going. He got to know that there were more similarities between the two religions and both had the same prophets. But as per Nizar's observance, many of the prophets in the Old Testament seem to be going out of favor with God and as they start getting older, richer or powerful, they seem to live a life which was not in accordance with what God had destined for them. But the prophets in the Holy Quran were always good and righteous. Kochu Daveed said, "What if the Holy Bible was saying the truth? It was probably giving a realistic picture of what these holy men became in their old age.

It is easy for men to go astray when they think they are God's own people and whatever they do must be right. These instances of Noah's drunkenness, David's adultery, and Solomon's harem and wealth can be shown as proof that though they were prophets, they were also human beings with their own short comings." Nizar smiled on hearing this and said, "I think God selected them as prophets and holy men only because of the strength of their character. We always try to portray the prophets as people of good character, who are not easily tempted by the vices of the world. Only then we could tell others to follow them and take them as an example." They both had some healthy discussions like this every day and Kochu Daveed started to feel at home in his new place.

Chapter 8

On the first Sunday of his arrival, Kochu Daveed went to church with Thomas. While coming back, Thomas casually asked him if he was getting too involved in religious discussions with Nizar. When he replied that he was interested in knowing more about different religions, Thomas said, "There is nothing wrong in that. But don't get attracted by the good façade presented to you. Every religion has its merits and demerits. It is a good thing to have a healthy outlook about other religions. But from what I hear from others, they think you are going to convert to Islam." He was stunned on hearing this. He replied after a moment of silence, "Cheta, I don't think I will abandon the religion practised by my parents and fore-fathers." Then he explained how he got interested in religious studies through his friendship with Fr. Nelson. It was Father who encouraged him to learn more and understand, instead of blindly following anything. Thomas was satisfied by his openness.

Since his conversation with Thomas he began to mingle more freely with everyone in the household. He didn't want them to think that he was only friendly with Nizar. He got to know more about them and one day he got a surprise gift from Reghu. It was a book called "Selected works of A.T Kovoor," which was translated into Malayalam. A.T. Kovoor was a famous rationalist who had taken on himself to expose the frauds of various Indian god-men and some organized religions. Once he started reading that book, he realised that he was now treading the waters in the other end of the religious spectrum. He got fascinated by the book and spent most of his time trying to read it. Nizar thought that he was avoiding him and decided to ask him directly about it. Kochu Daveed denied having any such thoughts and told him about the new book he was reading. Nizar said that he had heard about that book and his religious teachers had told him not to read such books which leads him away from God. Kochu Daveed smiled and said. "If your beliefs are strong and has a strong foundation, nothing is going to make cracks on that." Nizar replied, "That is true. But it is my duty to protect my beliefs and see that it is not unduly shaken."

Next Sunday Nizar left early in the morning and he returned only in the evening. Before bedtime while they were sitting and talking in the verandah, Nizar gave him the book of Holy Quran with Malayalam translation. Kochu Daveed was happy on receiving that. Next evening he got another surprise, Ouseph Chetan gave him his old Bible saying, "I see that you have other books. I am not a very religious person. But I don't want a good Christian to be misled by other people. Keep this with you as a stronghold in times of turbulence." Seeing the otherwise silent Ouseph Chetan trying to protect him, Kochu Daveed was really moved to tears. Before sleeping he went near the bed of Ouseph and said," Don't worry Cheta, I will not bring shame on my parents or my upbringing."

The days after that were going very fast for Kochu Daveed. He was improving a lot in his workplace. He was able to do most of the work that was expected from him. He always tried to do more than that. Though he was supposed to help Ouseph Chetan, he helped others also. Everyone treated him like their younger brother and being the youngest in the team he respected everyone. Evenings were spent in discussions with Nizar and Reghu. He always kept the discussions in a neutral manner to not offend any listeners. He was ready to accept the good points put forward by anyone if there was a logic in their presentation.

He continued with his daily rosary. But before the prayers he always found time to read one of the three books he had with him. He found the claim of Nizar that the Holy Quran was more appropriate for anyone to read was true. He had a sudden irreverent thought that if the Holy Bible was subjected to censorship now, it would have been restricted to adults only. He now understood why some of the Christian denominations try to distribute only the New Testament. New Testament can be read by anyone, as the life of Jesus and his apostles were quite exemplary.

Daveed's journey through the Holy Quran was going through well with the help of Nizar. Nizar explained the circumstances when each of the Surahs were sent down by God through the Prophet. He liked the first chapter in the Holy Quran, Al Fatihah, which is essentially a prayer for guidance and mercy of God. Nizar explained that this prayer is always paired with other prayers during their namaz times.

Thomas called him to his room on the first of the month and told him that he is now eligible for his first salary. The amount he gave him was far more than he had expected and more than he used to get from his previous jobs in Kochi. He told him that he needs to clear his dues the next day in the tea shop where they have their breakfast and lunch. Kochu Daveed gave him back half the amount and told him to save it for him. He then asked him if he could show him a post office from where he could send some amount as money order to his mother. He planned to write a few words in the money order form itself, just to let her know that he is well and safe here. The next day during lunch time, Thomas took him to the post office, and he sent the money as planned. He bought a pair of inland letter sheets for later use. He thought he would write his mother a longer letter just to make her feel that everything in going good here. Thomas took him to a bank on their way back and made him open a savings account. He deposited the remaining amount into his account and gave him the passbook. This was the first time he was entering a bank and he felt that his life is taking a turn to better at last. He asked Thomas about the expenses of the supper at home and if he must share the rent of the house they are staying. Thomas said that those things are taken care of by him, he need not worry about it.

He was happy to work with such a nice group of people. His respect for the group grew during the holy month of Ramadhan. Nizar started his obligatory fasting in that month. He woke up earlier than usual and prepared his food to eat before sunrise and he didn't eat or drink anything till sunset. Thomas told everyone before the fasting period started that he will be allowing Nizar to leave work at 4.00 p.m. so that he could get ready to break his fast at home. He also took care not to give Nizar too much heavy work during that time. Nizar told him that he need not give him any special consideration. But everyone including Thomas took care of him like their own brother. During this month there was not much time for religious discussions, and everyone took care not to eat or drink in front of Nizar. He was in his room most of the free time reading his Holy Quran. Kochu Daveed was really impressed by the fervour with which Nizar followed his religious principles.

It was during this time that he came to interact more with Reghu. During his conversations with Reghu, he came to know that he is from a poor family. His father used to be a loading/unloading worker in Cochin Port. He was a local leader of the workers' trade union, affiliated to the Communist Party of India, fighting for the rights of his co-workers. He got involved in some political rivalry with some other trade union workers and in the ensuing melee, he got injured in the head and after a long stay in the hospital, succumbed to his injuries. Reghu's elder brother got a job in the Port as a dependant of the dead leader. Reghu was deeply affected by his father's death and he started to get involved in the political party of his father. He became the rebellious middle son, always getting into fights. Fearing for his life, his mother took him to Mr. Thomas, his father's old friend, who took him under his wings and gave him a stable life. His old political affiliations and his father's death made him an atheist. He liked to quote Karl Marx, "Religion is an opiate for the masses." He had a collection of many books from rational authors translated into Malayalam. His favorite subject was the theory of evolution by Charles Darwin.

Kochu Daveed was open to discussion with Reghu on the theory of evolution, but he was not convinced that everything just came into being without any creator. He was ready to accept that the story of Genesis as told in the Old Testament has lots of loopholes. It could not be corelated with the scientific facts that were known at that time. But Reghu was not able to put forth any possible explanations on how the chemicals that were found in the earth were able to combine and form a living cell. Though they discussed many things they were not able to reach an amicable conclusion. They both knew that they didn't have that much knowledge about these things. So, in the end there was no argument or heartaches. Kochu Daveed decided that when he had enough money, he would at least try to buy some good books and increase his knowledge.

By the end of the Ramadhan month, Kochu Daveed had a clear idea of where his loyalties laid as far as religion was concerned. He considered Nizar to be an ideal religious man, not bothered about what others are thinking, but steadfast in his following of the teachings of his religion. His belief was complete, and he didn't have any doubts and so he was confident about what he was following. Reghu on the other hand was just against all religions and was not sure in what he believed. Kochu Daveed knew that he would not be able to be a believer like Nizar or be against everything like Reghu. His stand was made clear on the day of Eid-ul-Fitr, the day after the Ramadhan fasting ended.

Eid-ul-Fitr was a holiday for everyone. Thomas bought mutton that day and everyone joined hands together to cook delicious mutton biriyani. After a lavish lunch, they all had a good nap. Nizar had told Kochu Daveed that he would take him to meet his friend in the evening. So, they both woke up early, got dressed and went to the next town. There they met Abdullah, an old friend of Nizar, who took them to his house. While having tea there, Nizar informed Abdullah that this is the friend to whom he gave the Holy Quran translated in Malayalam. Then Abdullah started asking him about his family and how much he knew about Islam. After talking for some time, he smiled and said, "Now, my dear friend, you are almost ready to convert to Islam. You would be a good convert with sound knowledge of our basic tenets. If you wish I could arrange to start the process." Though taken aback by this sudden turn of events, Kochu Daveed was composed when he replied, "I think I am not ready yet. Moreover, decisions like this will be taken only after I discuss with my parents. I don't want to spring any surprises on them."

Abdullah looked and Nizar, smiled and said, "Don't worry about your parents. We know by experience that no parent would willingly accept their child converting to another religion. You must take a bold step forward and your parents will follow you. This is all for the Glory of God and if it is His Will, it will happen. All you need to think about is how to become a good Muslim and set a goal to perform the ultimate act of belief, The Hajj." Kochu Daveed then asked, "What if my parents and my family don't follow me?" "Maybe not immediately," Abdullah replied, "But they will come when they see that you are strong in your belief. Till that time, we will be your parents given by God the Almighty." "No need to decide anything today," he continued, "take your time. We will always be ready to welcome you."

They did not talk much on their way back to their home. Before they entered their house, Nizar said, "I didn't expect Abdullah to talk to you like this today. Please don't think that I am forcing anything on you. Whatever your decision, I will accept it and be friends with you like before. And please do not discuss this with anyone in the house." He agreed and they both went back to their respective rooms. With his mind in turmoil, Kochu Daveed tried to sleep, but he couldn't. The words of Abdullah rang in his ears loud and clear. He wondered if the friendship shown by Nizar was just a means of getting him to convert to his religion. But on second thoughts, he decided that Nizar is too genuine to think like that. He might be the one who was giving wrong signals to Nizar by his enthusiasm to the teachings of his religion. He fell into a troubled sleep and next day morning he looked so tired and sick that Thomas told him to stay home and take rest. The work in the sub-contract was coming to an end and they were almost finished with the remaining jobs.

In the evening he was feeling a lot better after a good day's rest. While having their supper, Thomas told them all to meet in his room after eating. When everyone was there, he announced that they will be staying there only for a week more. He already has a contract to work in an oxygen producing unit in Madras called the Indian Oxygen Limited. That work might take a year to finish and it was inside their manufacturing unit. Whoever is willing to come to Madras can come. Everyone can go home, meet their families and reach Madras in two weeks time. All were happy on hearing the news. Kochu Daveed stayed back after everyone left and asked, "Cheta, is it okay with you if I go straight to Madras? I don't want to go and meet my parents yet. I have not reached my goal. I want to go home as a winner, a hero, not the one who is still in the growing stage." Thomas smiled and agreed to it. He said he would talk about it later when the time comes to move out.

Chapter 9

A week went by very fast. Everyone was excited to go home and meet their families. When he saw the excitement of everyone, he too wanted to go home to see his mother. But the thought of his father's reaction if he went home empty handed made him strong in his resolution. He would go home only when he has a good address to talk of. He did not want to be known as the guy working in a small workshop. If someone asks him, he should be able to say the name of a big company as his employer.

His friendship with Nizar and Reghu was as strong as before. Though Nizar had felt a little bad in the beginning, they overcame that awkwardness. A good conversation between them cleared all their misunderstandings. Kochu Daveed made it quite clear that though he would like to discuss about religions, he was not ready to convert to any other religions, including atheism. He was open to criticism and was ready to accept that his church had made mistakes. But he pointed out that any religion was in its pure form only when its founder was alive. Later, when the number of followers increase, the number of leaders also increase, leading to different interpretations of the original teachings. When the number of followers exceed a certain point, splits happen within and a new group is formed. It is the same with other groups too. The three friends agreed to respect each other's opinions and go forward as friends.

On the last day, Thomas called aside Kochu Daveed, gave him a train ticket to Madras and the address of the Indian Oxygen Limited company. He told him to find a cheap lodging near to that company and stay there for a week. He would come and meet him after a week. Since all of them were going to meet again in a week's time, there were no teary goodbyes. From Visakapattnam station everyone went their own ways.

Kochu Daveed reached Madras Central station early in the morning, the next day. Madras is the capital of the State of Tamilnadu and is one of the four metro cities in India. The language spoken here is Tamil, which is one of the oldest languages. Though the language was new to him, his experience in other language speaking areas made him comfortable in facing anything. Moreover, his own native language, Malayalam was derived from Tamil. So, he was confident that he would be able to communicate well here. As usual, with a prayer in his heart, he stepped out of the railway station and hailed a rickshaw to take him to the place called Tondiarpet, where the Indian Oxygen Ltd. was situated. Once he reached there, he went around the area looking for a cheap lodge, where he could stay for a week. After some walking around, he found one and though the manager of that place was not willing at first to give a room to him because he looked different from the locals, he relented when Kochu Daveed was willing to pay one week's rent in advance.

After he made himself fresh, he went outside looking for a place to eat and to have a look around the city. He found the main bus stand in that area and decided to get familiar with the city in one week. The one good thing he found was that all the names of the bus routes were written in Tamil and English, which made it easier for him to get into the right bus. With a mixture of English and Malayalam, he was able to communicate with the boy who was handling the front desk in the lodge. From him he came to know about the important places to visit in Madras. The Marina Beach is the second longest beach in the world and as per the front desk boy, that should be the first one to see. At one end of the beach there is the Anna Samadhi, which is the memorial built for the former Chief Minister of Tamilnadu, C.N Annadurai, who was cremated there. Nearby is the Santhome Cathedral, built by the Portuguese. Then there are forts built by the British, old marketplaces, and famous temples. Being a Christian, he was also told to visit the St. Thomas Mount where, one of the disciples of Jesus Christ, St. Thomas, was believed to have spent his last days and killed there by the king's soldiers.

With so much details in hand, Kochu Daveed decided to spend his days looking around the city, till the arrival of Thomas. Within a few days he understood one important aspect of Tamilian character. They were fiercely loyal to their language, Tamil. They were proud of the fact that their language was considered one of the oldest languages in the world and they were not ready to give importance to any other language than their own. They had fiercely agitated against the imposition of Hindi as the national language of India, even before the independence of India from the British rule. Even after the Indian independence, when the Central Government tried to bring in Hindi as an official language and tried to impose it on all the southern states, the people of Tamilnadu, irrespective of the age and gender took to the streets against it and after lots of rioting and loss of lives, the Central Government had to retreat from their stand. Tamilnadu is the only state in India where Hindi is not taught in schools.

After a week of going around the city, Kochu Daveed was getting restless. He did not receive any message from Thomas, and he had no idea about how to contact him. On the tenth morning, while he was coming out after breakfast, he saw Thomas standing on the street corner and trying to decide which way to go. He ran to Thomas and called, "Cheta, I am here!" Thomas looked around and saw him. He said. "I knew you would be around this place. That was why I was waiting here. Come, let us go to the place I have rented here." He went back to the lodging and vacated the room. Together they went to the new place which was just walkable distance to the Indian Oxygen Ltd. In an elongated plot of land, there were five houses built in a row, one behind the other. The last house was occupied by the landlord. Thomas had rented the first house which was bigger compared to others. It had four rooms and a kitchen, with the bathroom behind the kitchen.

Within two days everyone was back from home and they started working as contractors in the Indian Oxygen Ltd. The work was expected to be at least a year long. They were working along with the erection team of the company and their main work was decided by them. They got to know the engineers in the team quite well and Kochu Daveed did his best to do whatever work he could. He soon got noticed by the head engineer of the erection group, Mr. Nambiar, who took a liking to this hard-working boy. He noticed that he was not only doing his work very well but was also eager to learn more about whatever was happening in the section.

Indian Oxygen Ltd. not only produced medical grade oxygen, but also other gases used for different purposes. They also erected oxygen and other gas lines in the hospitals and other big institutions. Mr. Nambiar was in-charge of these operations and he used to be in different parts of the country overseeing the projects. He normally hired people for different contracts and takes them with him. One day he casually asked Kochu Daveed if he was interested in working with him in his next contract. Kochu Daveed said that he would discuss with Thomas Chetan and inform him next day.

In the evening, he went and talked to Thomas. He said, "Mr. Nambiar asked me if I would like to go with him in his next contract job in Mysore. What should I say?" Thomas asked him, "What is your opinion?" He replied, "I think it is not really better than what I am doing now. I will still be a contract worker." "That's right, I am glad that you were able to think like that. I will talk to him tomorrow and see if he will be able to make you an employee of Indian Oxygen Ltd. in the future. Then it would be good for you." On hearing this Kochu Daveed was happy that he went and discussed this matter with Thomas. He knew Thomas would do what is good for him and he had this strong belief that God will guide him through the right path.

The next day he saw Thomas talking with Mr. Nambiar and they parted in a friendly way. On the way back, Mr. Nambiar smiled at him and said, "You are a smart boy." He didn't understand what he meant but thought that it was a good sign. In the evening Thomas called him and said, "I talked to Mr. Nambiar and we arranged that you will be with me till our work here is over. After that he will take you with him in his next contract job and he assured me that he would like to make you an employee of Indian Oxygen Ltd." He was happy on hearing this and decided that he would go back to his mother only when he became an employee of the Indian Oxygen Ltd.

Life in Madras seemed to go very fast. The friendship with his colleagues was in a good standing and everyone was happy to know that his life was going forward in a better way. He never missed his daily prayers and rosary. His earlier enthusiasm to get to know more about other religions cooled down a bit after the conversion drama. Each one of them went their own way for the time being. With the impending change in direction of his life, he regretted not continuing his school studies. So, with the help of Thomas and Nambiar he started looking out for basic technical books which he thought would help him later. Used books were available in the Moore Market near the Central railway station. He became a regular visitor there every weekend. Nambiar had suggested that he improve his English and basic Mathematics. With that in mind he started buying old school textbooks of English and Maths. Though he found learning English tough, he was surprised to know that he enjoyed learning Maths. He was able to solve the high school level problems, which made him regret dropping out of school.

A year went by quickly and it was time for him to separate from his friends. Kochu Daveed had started sending small amounts of money regularly to his mother and they kept in touch through letters every fortnight. His mother wanted him to visit them once his contract was over, but he told that he would come only when he gets a permanent job. From his mother's letters he came to know that they were looking for an alliance for his second sister and she too will be getting married soon. Now his only prayer was that he gets the promised job with Indian Oxygen Ltd. before his sister gets married.

When Thomas and his roommates left Madras, he got himself a single room in one of the housing complexes where they allowed bachelors to stay. He started to work with Mr. Nambiar immediately and when he expressed his desire to go home for his sister's wedding, he was told to give him two weeks' notice so that he could arrange someone for a month. When he asked about the permanent job in the company, Nambiar smiled and said that he had started moving his papers and it will be known soon. He need not worry about anything. One of the younger engineers in the group had agreed to take him under his wings and teach him all about systems and drawings.

At last he got a letter from his mother saying that his sister's wedding was finalised with an ex-service man, who was now into farming in the beautiful town of Alappuzha. Time had come for him to return home. Mr. Nambiar assured that by the time he would be returning from Kochi, his job in Indian Oxygen Ltd. will be waiting for him. He was elated to hear about his job from Mr. Nambiar. After the initial elation he had a moment of disquiet when he started to think about meeting his parents after a long time. He knew that his mother would be her old loving self, but he was unsure about the reaction from his father. Though his mother did not write much about his father in her letters, other than he is well and improving, he was not sure if there was any noticeable change in him.

He decided to take all his savings from the bank and after doing a bit of shopping, mainly clothes, he drew a demand draft for the balance amount on the advice of Mr. Nambiar. As the date of return began to near, he was feeling a bit jittery and at the same time excited about his meeting with his family. At last he got into the Cochin Express heading towards Cochin Harbour Terminus. Though it was an overnight travel, he knew he would not sleep because of his excitement. He lay on his berth thinking of the day he left Kochi and the path his life had taken till now. He understood that it was not his ability or expertise that took him to the level he is now, but God's Grace alone which had guided him so far. He was thankful and grateful for all the mercy shown by God till that day. He kept saying prayers of thankfulness whenever he thought of this. The next day, early morning he set foot back in his hometown after a gap of more than two years. He had not informed anyone of his arrival. So, he did not expect anyone to receive him at the station. He wanted to keep his visit a surprise. He came out of the railway station and hailed a taxi to take him home.

Chapter 10

When the taxi stopped in front of the gate, the first one to notice him was his close friend and neighbour Pappu, who ran out and hugged him. Pappu's family had a small grocery store and Kochu Daveed remembered with gratefulness the times when Pappu would steal small animal-shaped biscuits which his mother used to make for selling and share with him when he was hungry. Pappu had a bigger grocery store now and he and his elder brother took care of it. He left the store with his brother and came to help Kochu Daveed pick his luggage and take them in to his house. When they opened the gate, its creaking sound was heard inside and his sisters came out to look who was coming. They saw Pappu coming in with the luggage and they ran to hug their brother. Hearing the commotion his mother came out of the kitchen and on seeing them, started crying tears of joy. She ran out and hugged him and took him inside the house. Pappu left after handing over the luggage and left the family who were shedding tears of happiness on the return of Kochu Daveed.

After the initial tears and laughter, his mother went to the kitchen to prepare breakfast for him. His sisters were asking him to open his suitcase so that they could see what gifts he had bought for them. He asked them about the whereabouts of his father and his mother heard him and said, "He has become a changed man now. He now goes to church every day early in the morning to attend mass, then has tea with his new friends from the tea shop in front of the church and returns home for breakfast. He then goes out and comes back for lunch. After lunch he takes a nap and, in the evening, goes for a walk till the beach and returns home before the family prayer. After prayers and supper, he goes to bed early." He then asked about his nemesis, Chandy and his alcoholic evenings. His mother replied, "Actually, all these changes in your father is because of Chandy. A few months back Chandy had a cardiac arrest and was hospitalised and his right side is partially paralysed. Doctors told him not to drink anymore. On seeing Chandy's condition, your father decided to restrict his drinking to Sundays only." He was happy on hearing this.

They heard the front gate creaking again and they saw his father coming in. He did look changed. He was wearing white dhoti and kurta with a big rosary around his neck. He was holding an umbrella like a walking stick and coming towards the house with steady steps. Kochu Daveed came out with folded palms and said, "Praise to Lord Jesus Christ." "Let the praise be for him always and forever" his father replied. Then he blessed him by placing his right palm on his head and smiled and said, "I had a hunch that you would come today. That is why I didn't stay there for tea and conversation with my friends." Then he turned to his wife and said, "Didn't I tell you yesterday to prepare some good food for today's breakfast? I knew he would come today." His mother smiled and said, "I was preparing to make appam and stew. It will be ready in a few minutes. By that time our daughter will prepare tea for everyone."

After a happy breakfast and tea, they all sat around the suitcases and Kochu Daveed opened it and gave out the gifts he brought for them. Then while the mother and daughters went to the kitchen to prepare lunch, his father gave him more details about the groom he had found for his second daughter. Then he asked him about his job and when he knew that he was going to start working in a proper company, he was very happy. After lunch of rice and fish curry they all had a nap. By evening he was fresh enough to go out and meet his friends.

The next day he went to Alappuzha to meet his would-be brother-in-law. He took his friend Pappu along with him. This guy, Peter, was a tough-looking guy but well mannered. Though they had gone there unannounced, they were welcomed warmly and given a good lunch. Kochu Daveed and Pappu came back impressed with the hard-working guy. He had taken over the farming from his ailing father and was able to run it successfully. He had no mother and he was clear in what he was expecting from his future wife. She should be able to be the lady of the house, support him in his efforts and take care of his elderly father. On returning home he informed his parents of his appreciation of his brother-in-law and made fun of his sister for taking charge of the husband's household which made her blush. He liked this new brother-in-law for his straightforward and no-nonsense approach.

Then they got busy with the wedding preparations, starting with invitations, which was going to each relatives' house and inviting them personally. Both father and son did that together. In those days, the custom was to invite everyone personally at least two weeks before the marriage and it was quite common to have enmity between families for a long time just because they were not invited properly according to the protocol. Kavungal Pathro's brothers were invited first, then the rest of the Kavungal family, followed by his wife's family and then the other relatives. During the long journeys, Kochu Daveed often wondered about the change in the attitude of his father. Did he really think that life is too short to waste time on alcohol? Or was he trying to repent for his past follies? He couldn't understand his father. But he liked the way he carried himself now.

A week before the wedding they started to raise an awning in front of their house to accommodate the guests coming for the wedding. At one corner they built a small stage big enough to seat the newly weds for the ceremonial cake cutting. They decorated the inside of the awning with colourful ribbons and on the day of the wedding they added fresh flowers in the decoration. The neighbours and friends pitched in to help with these activities. They arranged to have tables and chairs to seat around a hundred people inside the awning. They also set up smaller tents for the people who will be waiting for the banquet.

Two days before the wedding, close relatives began to arrive and, in the night, everyone adjusted and slept wherever they could. Most of the men slept on the tables set inside the awning. Everything went as per plan and the wedding was a grand success as far as Kochu Daveed was concerned. The bride and groom stayed there for their customary three days and were sent off with tears and gifts on the fourth day to the groom's house. The groom was a little miffed that people were more interested in talking to Kochu Daveed than him. But he understood the reason for it. He too had heard good things about his brother-in-law. How he had run away from home and returned with a good job in a reputed company.

Kavungal Pathro and his wife were very relieved when all the festivities were over. They sighed in relief after they were able to marry off their second daughter. They had to sell some more land to give enough money as dowry and for the marriage expenses. But they were happy that Kochu Daveed was able to help them in whatever way he could. For the first time in his life, Kochu Daveed felt that his father was proud of him. During this short period, he had heard many times his father talking very highly about him and his new job in Madras to his relatives. So much so, he heard from his mother that he was getting marriage proposals from many of his distant relatives. He told her that he would like to wait for his younger sister also to get settled and then he would think of marrying. He thought that this would stop his mother from pursuing that matter. But he was wrong in that.

A day after the bride and groom returned to their home, during the family supper, his father asked him directly about his marriage. Though he was taken aback from this sudden question, he managed to reply that he would wait till his youngest sister got married. But his father replied, "That would still take at least two to three years. Since you have a good job now, it is wise to start looking for a good alliance. I am not saying that you marry this year itself. We will plan it for next year, but we should start looking for a good girl from a good family." He did not have anything to counter his father's logic. So, he said, "I have to return to work this week. You both can start looking for a nice girl but do not be in a hurry. I will be able to take a day or two of leave of absence only after my six months' probation period. Once you have decided on a good family and you both like the girl, I will come and visit them after that." They agreed to his plan.

Daveed returned to Madras that weekend. He got himself a small room for a month in his old lodging place and reported to work in Mr. Nambiar's office on Monday morning. Nambiar introduced him to his other colleagues and assigned him to the youngest engineer of his team, Mr. Maheshwaran. He was a tall, lanky guy, very dark in complexion but with a pleasant face. He smiled at him when he called him "Sir." He told him, "Please don't call me Sir. Just call me Mahesh. I may be just few years older than you and this is my first job." Kochu Daveed decided that he would get to like this guy very much. Nambiar said, "Mahesh has a diploma in Mechanical Engineering. Learn whatever you can from him. He has good knowledge and he will teach you well." "Your first project will be in Davangere in Karnataka State. You will be able to get ready in a week with your tools and enough men. Mahesh will lead you all. It is not a big job. It should last about three months. It is in the new hospital they are building now. Mahesh will be sending daily progress reports to me. Be with him and learn how to do that too."

He was happy to go to a new place with his new group. He followed Mahesh like a shadow and learnt many things from him. He took interest in doing not only what he was told, but also tried to understand the basic process of what they were doing. He was not afraid to ask questions when he did not understand something, and Mahesh patiently explained to him everything. By the time their work was completed in Davangare, he understood where he was lacking in technical aspects of the work and decided to learn more about it. On his return, he discussed with Nambiar and Mahesh on how he could improve his knowledge. They suggested that he take some evening classes in a nearby Industrial Training Centre (ITC) and get some basic knowledge about engineering. Those classes are meant for people like him, who have not graduated from high school. There he could get some hands-on training on different aspects and learn how to do some basic engineering drawings. They told him that it was better to start investing on his personal development, which would benefit him in the future.

Daveed took to the class like fish to water and he spent all his free time trying to study something new. His whole life started to revolve around his workplace and classes. He still found time to write to his mother and continue his daily prayers. His mother's letters always included details of some girl they had gone to see for him and how they thought she was not fit for him. He read through them with a knowing smile. He knew that the main "fit" his parents were looking at was about his height. He was the shortest in the family and the task was to find a short girl to match him.

Another short project saw him travel to Hubli in Karnataka State with Mahesh and team again. On his return he found a letter from his mother saying that they found a girl for him. The proposal was brought by his father's cousin, Eliamma,who lives in Alapuzha. The girl is her husband's brother's daughter. They had gone to see her and liked the way she looked and behaved. Their family is good, a bit higher in status than them. Another good thing is that they think she is shorter than him, at least not taller than him. She has completed her Pre-degree course and though she wanted to study even further, her parents think that it is time to marry her off. So, he replied to them saying that he could come home for a week if he could combine the weekend and a holiday falling on a Thursday, the following month. With the permission of Mr. Nambiar and Mahesh, he started his journey back home to see if he could find his future life partner.

When he was on the train returning home, a sudden thought crossed his mind. What if he didn't like the girl. His mother had not sent him any picture of the girl and from the way his mother was describing her, he knew that they liked her. He just hoped that his mother would have an idea about his likes and dislikes. He hoped that he would not be an embarrassment to his family. Then he thought, what if the girl didn't like him. Though she might be shorter than him, she could still prefer taller men. With these conflicting thoughts he was not able to sleep properly in the train and he was all tired and sleepy by the time he reached home. His family was happy that he had come as they had wished, and they started to arrange for a formal visit to the girl's house.

Chapter 11

The girl was from the Kottaram valappil family. Kottaram valappil means 'in the compound of the King's palace'. As the name signifies, in olden days they used to live in the premises of the King's palace; probably some high-ranking officials in the palace. They did own large areas of land, possibly gifted by the King and as time went by and monarchy ended, they managed to get good positions in other private companies due to their better educational qualifications. At the time of the story, the family consisted of four brothers and their immediate families. The girl's father, Yohannan, was the eldest among the brothers and he worked as a manager in a large tea exporting firm. The second brother, Mathai, a high-ranking army official who took a voluntary retirement and later took up a job as a high school teacher, lived with his family in the adjacent plot. The third brother was a little away from these two and lived near the Shavakkotta Bridge with his family, while the last brother sold off his property and moved to Kochi near his wife's house. The bond between Yohannan and Mathai was more like friends than brothers. They lived with their family next to each other and because of their closeness, both their families were also very close to each other. Yohannan had four sons and two daughters, whereas Mathai had three sons and four daughters. Their houses were built on large plots of over an acre each and there was only a natural boundary of trees between their plots. All the thirteen kids played together, went to school together and could always be seen together everywhere.

In the evenings, it was usual to find all the kids playing in the space between their houses, which were full of coconut and areca nut palms, mango, guava, jackfruit and other trees. In one of the shades we could always see the two brothers sitting on their cane chairs, sipping tea and sharing their daily experiences, while the women of the house prepared supper. They had enough maids to help them around the house and they all lived a very happy and peaceful life, which at times was slightly disturbed by the unnecessary ego issues of Eliamma, who was from the Kavungal family in Kochi. She was the cousin of Kavungal Pathro. But the brothers made sure that the occasional disturbances in their peaceful existence did not affect their loving relationship. One of the main grievances of Eliamma was that he gave more importance to his brother than his wife. Any important news was shared with the elder brother first. All others came only second to that relation. That attitude made her feel resentment towards Yohannan, which sometimes went out of control, ending in a verbal duel between Mathai and his wife, in the end of which Yohannan had to interfere to make peace between them.

Theresa the youngest of Yohannan's children was the naughtiest and almost tomboyish in nature. She was ready to challenge anyone in any games and competing with the elder boys of her family, made her act like a boy most of the time. Being the second youngest in the group and protected by her big brothers made her bold and fearless. When she was not playing with her siblings, she was either reading or painting. When the four girls got together, she was the natural leader of the group. She went around both the houses like a butterfly, singing and dancing and making everyone happy. By the time the kids went on to become teenagers and above, the boys and the girls started to go their separate ways as a group. It was at that time that Yohannan's wife's mother sent her a new maid along with her fatherless teenaged daughter. Her name was Molly and she was a slender, beautiful girl with melancholic eyes. All the boys in the household wanted to be her knight in shining armour but she had eyes only for the most silent and soft-spoken second eldest brother of Theresa named Michael. Michael was also Theresa's favorite brother.

Theresa understood that Michael and Molly were in love with each other and it showed so clearly in their behavior that everyone except their parents noticed it. The brothers always made fun of him but kept it a secret from their parents. It was during this time that Yohannan's eldest son Joseph decided that he had enough of studies. He had completed his first year in degree class and thought that he could not study anymore. His father, using his influence, got him a job as a supervisor in their sister concern dealing with rubber products. As per the custom of that time, he was soon in demand in the marriage market as a most eligible bachelor. His marriage was arranged very soon, and he got married to a girl from Kottayam. They were given a separate room in the house, which made Molly sleep in the room of Theresa and her sister. With the elder brother sharing the expenses of the household, and with a scheming wife by his side, he soon became the de facto head of the house. Even though Yohannan was still working, he had trouble with his eyesight, which made him depend on his eldest son for all kinds of transactions in the house. Joseph started handling all the revenue coming out of their paddy farms and coconut plantations.

The second son, Michael, started his own painting contracting firm and when he started to earn enough money to maintain a household, he went and asked his father permission to marry Molly. Though his father and mother were shocked on hearing this, they agreed. But his brothers and sisters thought that he was marrying someone beneath his status and made it clear that they would not be happy to live with Molly as their sister-in-law. This made Michael sad. He had thought that his siblings would understand his true love. So, he decided to move out of the house with his wife to a different city and start his painting contract there.

The other two brothers of Theresa were not very ambitious. They were happy to get their pocket money, spend it on gambling in different card clubs, win sometimes and lose sometimes, return home by night, have supper and sleep peacefully. Theresa was sad to see her once happy and boisterous family disintegrating into a silent empty shell. The situation was not very different in the household of Mathai. Their kids were also just content on enjoying their family's wealth and not do anything worthwhile. Mathai's family had another reason to be in a perpetual unhappy state. He lost his eldest daughter, Mariam, while she was at school. She was tall and graceful but not good in studies. She normally towered over her classmates which made her an easy target for jokes. One day she missed her homework and her teacher made her stand outside her classroom the whole day. She was told that she would be allowed in to the class only when she brings her father to school. But she was afraid to inform her father and so she suffered the humiliation of standing outside the class for a whole week. When the teacher saw that she was adamant, she stepped up her punishment one more level and made her stand outside the school and sent a note to Mariam's father through another cousin of hers. This was too much to bear for young Mariam and that night she dressed herself in white saree and walked in to the sea.

One early morning when everyone woke up, they could not find the eldest daughter of Mathai anywhere. At first, they thought that she must have gone to Theresa's house because they were very close friends too. But they started to panic when they couldn't find her there and Theresa had no idea where she was. Everyone in both the household went around to different areas searching for her. By afternoon someone came and told them that a fisherman had seen her in the beach near the famous sea bridge of Alapuzha. On hearing this Mathai's mother and others started crying, intuitively knowing that she must have drowned in the sea. Some local fishermen took out their rowing boats and went out to sea in search for her. But an old fisherman sitting in front of his hut told his grandson, "No use looking for her now. When the Sea Mother takes away something, she will return it only after three days". However, unlike his prediction, her body was washed ashore the same day in a deserted beach towards the south.

The death of his eldest daughter brought a big change in Mathai. He became a recluse, stopped going to school, took a long leave of absence and stayed at home. For more than a year there was no festivities in both the houses. There was total silence in both the households, everyone taking refuge in their own private rooms and not willing to come out and talk to others. Theresa started having strange nightmares where she always saw her dead cousin calling her to follow her. Many a times she was found sleepwalking in the night and when she woke up she always told them that she is holding hands and walking with her cousin.

Yohannan and his wife took her to the parish priest daily, who sprinkled blessed water on her and prayed for the release of any evil spirits from her body. She was also given a rosary blessed by the Pope and told to wear it always. They also made her sleep in her parents' room and slowly she got over her trauma. She stopped going to college and started staying at home and reading a lot of books borrowed from the library.

After a year, her elder sister got married to a farmer in Cherthala and she was left alone in the house. By that time both Yohannan and his wife were having health issues. Yohannan's eyesight was becoming poorer and his wife was having problems with her kidney functions. Their eldest son, Joseph, became the sole bread winner of the family. It was not that they were depending only on his income. The revenue from the crops were also coming in, but Joseph oversaw everything. The two younger brothers were still not ready to take any responsibilities and Joseph liked it that way. They were given monthly allowances, which they spent on whatever they wanted and by the end of the month they took advance from the next month's allowance. Joseph's wife kept a good account book for them alone.

Theresa had only her three remaining cousin sisters as friends and one day she decided to resume her studies. She took permission from her parents and her brother and sister-in-law and took admission for the degree class in St. Joseph's College for women, with English literature as her main subject. That brought her into the world of literary giants like Charles Dickens, Jane Austen, Hemingway, Chesterton, Arthur Conan Doyle and others. More than the classes, it was the library that interested her. She read books, whatever she could lay hands on, the whole day. Sitting in her room, she imagined herself to be the main character in the book that she was reading, especially if it was a book by Jane Austen. She dreamed that some romance like that would happen in her life too.

But life does not happen the way it does in the books. It takes its twists and turns on its own. Her mother's health began to fail and she had to miss classes to take care of her. But that did not stop her from reading. Even while sitting with her mother, she managed to read when her mother was tired and sleeping. It was during that time that Yohannan started to think of finding a good groom for her. He wanted to settle her with some nice guy before his time comes to an end. Theresa wanted to complete her degree before her marriage, but her parents managed to convince her that they would like to see her settled in life before something happens to them. They discussed this with Mathai and family. Mathai's wife immediately informed them that she knew a good, hard-working boy, who is also her cousin's son from Kochi. She said that she saw him recently during the wedding of his sister and knew that he was working in a big company in Madras. She would vouch for the character of that boy. They did not need any more assurances. They told her to proceed with arranging a good time to meet the groom and his family.

The next day Mathai's wife, with the help of her eldest son, went to see Kavungal Pathro in Kochi. They caught the early morning bus and reached there before noon. Pathro and his wife were surprised on seeing them. But they recovered quickly, invited them inside and gave them tender coconut water to drink. Then she went and called her neighbour's son and with his help caught one of her roosters and asked him to get it ready for lunch. After a delicious lunch with chicken curry and rice, Mathai's wife came to the point quickly. Kochu Daveed's mother was happy with the proposal, but Pathro wanted to know if his son would get enough dowry from that family. Mathai's wife explained to him that though the family is now run by the eldest son, Joseph, they had already bought enough gold for their last daughter and moreover when the family property is up for partition, every child would get an appropriate share. Pathro was satisfied with that. So, they decided on a date to first come and see Theresa and if they liked her, they would inform Kochu Daveed who would come and finalize the wedding date and time. Everything went on as planned. Pathro and his wife liked the girl. They had taken a picture of Kochu Daveed with them to show it to the girl's family. On returning home they wrote a letter to Kochu Daveed to come and proceed with the wedding preparations.

Chapter 12

The day after Kochu Daveed reached home in Kochi, his father went to the local post office and from there made a call to Theresa's brother Joseph's office. He informed him that his son is now in Kochi and asked if it was possible to arrange for a meeting between the boy and the girl. Joseph said that they would be happy to arrange the meeting on the following Saturday. He told him that they would be expecting all of them for lunch also. Pathro came home and informed everyone about Saturday's plan. Kochu Daveed was worried that it was going too fast. He had not even seen the girl, they had not even given a picture and they were already talking about having lunch there, in the hope that everything is going to be decided that day. He shared his doubts with his mother who smiled and said, "Don't worry. We have seen the girl. She will be perfect for you. I know you will like her. We just need to decide on a date and time." He was comforted by his mother's words, but at the back of his mind he was thinking, "What if the girl doesn't like me? I am not as tall as my father. What if I am shorter than her? She will definitely not like that." He didn't know who he could turn to for an advice. He went and discussed with his best friend Pappu. But the only idea Pappu had was to wear shoes with higher heels. But that idea was helpful only if they were outside the house. Everyone normally leaves their footwear outside when entering any house. At last he decided to go and face it. If the girl didn't like him, he would take it as an excuse to not to come home for a year and thereby getting a break from this marriage drama.

Unknown to him, the same discussion was going on Theresa's household also. Theresa had come to know from her aunt that the proposed groom is not as tall as his father. She had told her two younger brothers, Thomas and John, about it and they had decided to measure the height of the boy when he comes to see their sister. They made her stand near the doorway and made a mark of her height using a piece of chalk. Their plan was to bring Kochu Daveed to that doorway somehow and see if he was taller than that mark. If he was too short, then they would device a plan to stop the marriage from taking place.

The day of the meeting arrived, and everything went on as planned. Their fears were all without any reason. Kochu Daveed liked the girl very much and Theresa was able to confirm that he was slightly taller than her. After lunch the elders sat around and finalized the dates for engagement and wedding ceremony. Kochu Daveed didn't get a chance to talk to the girl alone, but he enjoyed the company of her brothers who took him around their farm. There was only one thing which he found quite jarring. They all were talking to him like he was making a lot of money in Madras. He understood that it must have been his father who might have given them an inflated idea of his earnings. He was debating whether he should correct that impression, but he didn't have the courage to do that. They all returned home with a feeling of mission accomplished. They had only three weeks to prepare for the wedding. So, they started planning the next day, which was a Sunday.

On Monday morning, Kochu Daveed called Mr. Nambiar and others and invited them to his wedding and asked Mahesh if he could find a good place for him to stay when he brings his wife to Madras. Mahesh said he would arrange that. Then he and his father started going around and inviting all their relatives and friends. They had to finish it within a week. The wedding would take place in the bride's parish church. Since they didn't have much time, they went and took the bishop's permission to waive one of the banns in the church. They also decided not to have an engagement ceremony to save some time.

All the neighbours and friends were invited for a dinner the day before the wedding. Only close relatives were invited to the wedding. They had given a list of one hundred people as the groom's group to the bride's family. So, they all rented two buses to go there and the groom and his parents rented a car to take them there. The wedding was a fairly well managed one with all the bride's relatives and cousins pitching in to help. The bride and groom stayed in the bride's house for three days as per the custom and then returned to Kochi.

Theresa was initially uncomfortable being in a new house with totally new people. But Kochu Daveed's youngest sister and mother made her feel comfortable and slowly she got used to their way of life. Within a week they had to go to Madras and she was more apprehensive of the life she was going to live there all alone without the help of any of her parents or siblings. She found that Kochu Daveed was a very private person, an introvert, spoke only when there was a need. But she on the other hand was an extrovert and she did not know how she would get along with him. She knew that she had no choice. He did tell his life story within the first few days after their marriage. From this, she gathered that she could trust him, he had a strong personality and was a very responsible person as a son, brother, and a husband. The only thing that bothered her was his lack of communication. She was a chatterbox, telling him whatever that came to mind, but he kept his thoughts to himself. But he was a good listener. So, she normally didn't mind him not speaking out.

On the day of her first journey outside Kerala, her brothers and sister-in-law came to see her off at the railway station. Since her parents were not well enough to travel, she had gone there one day and taken leave from them. When the train started moving, she suddenly felt very lonely and started crying. Kochu Daveed took her in his arms and comforted her. She cried on his shoulders for a long time and then fell asleep due to exhaustion. Mahesh was there at the station to receive them and he took them to a small house he had rented for them in Amman Kovil Street. The house was a small portion of a large mansion which was divided into smaller portions for renting purposes. They had rented a part with one small living room, a bedroom and a kitchen arranged in a line. The bathroom and toilet were at the end of the line after the kitchen. There were three other families in that big mansion, and each had their own private area. The big hall in the centre of the mansion was common to everyone.

Kochu Daveed stayed home the first day to arrange everything in their new house. Mahesh had done a good job of getting all the required things in the house. Together they went and introduced themselves in the evening to the other renters in the house. In one portion was an older couple with a teenaged son named Gopi. They looked older for a teenage son but Kochu Daveed later came to know that they had adopted Gopi after a long time of childless agony. Theresa took a liking to Gopi's mother who reminded her of her own mother. She started calling her Gopiamma (meaning Gopi's mother). Gopi's father worked in a medical store. The next portion had a younger couple with two small kids, Shanker and Meena, aged five and three years. The father worked in a small factory. The third portion was occupied by a couple, who were not very friendly people. Others told the newcomers that it was best not to be in touch with the couple in the third portion. The rumour was that they are not really a legal couple, but the man's paramour and he doesn't like anyone talking to that lady. The lady also doesn't come out of the house often. Everyone sees them when they are going out and returning together.

Theresa being an extrovert was soon in good company with Gopiamma and Shankar's mother. They sat and chatted in the afternoons in the common hall when their husbands were at work. Since she was used to having maids to do the cooking at her home, she struggled initially to prepare even the basic meals of the day. Kochu Daveed was very understanding and he did not complain. He showed her whatever he knew about cooking, the stuff he learned when staying with his roommates earlier. Theresa wrote to her sister-in-law to send her some good Kerala recipes and learnt a lot from her two neighbours. On the first of the month she saw that the salary slip her husband showed her was not what she expected. Her first thought was that he cheated her family by giving them an inflated figure in salary, but on pondering over it, she decided to give him a benefit of doubt. From the behaviour she had been seeing so far, he did not seem to be crooked. She thought of asking him directly about it, but then decided against it. She was little worried when he started to write down how he was going to spend the money. A part of it was going to his parents. Then they must pay the rent and part of the electricity bill. She must manage the household expenses with the remaining amount. She saw that she had to be careful with how she spends the money. On seeing the look of consternation in her face, Kochu Daveed said, "I think that you were expecting more. This is what I get every month. But you need not worry. On the weeks I am on tour, I get extra allowances which will help us." She was stunned on hearing that he would be on tour frequently. Then she might have to live alone in this strange place. She expressed her fears to him, and he replied, "I will check with Mr. Nambiar if I could take you with me for until you get used to this place." She was relieved on hearing that.

He kept his word and took her with him when he had work outside the state. She got a chance to stay in Orissa, Pondicherry, Vellore, and Bangalore. She was happy to meet her brother and family in Bangalore. Soon she was able to handle all the finances of the household with the income and was still able to save some amount for a rainy day. When he saw that she was getting bored while he was at work, he took her to the used books store in Moore Market where they bargained with the shopkeeper and managed to buy lots of old English novels. This made her happier. She was content with looking after the household needs and then reading whenever she was free. In the evenings when he returned from work, she was happy serving him what she learned to cook that day and kept a lively chatter of the day's happening. Into this peaceful life two incidents happened which shattered their peace of mind.

One evening they were having tea and snacks in their living room when they heard a commotion outside. They went out to see what happened and saw that a verbal duel was going on with the tough guy in the third portion and Gopi's parents. They understood from their shouting that Gopi had gone and knocked at the guy's house when he was not there. He had gone to give them a letter, which was dropped at Gopi's house by mistake. But the man mistook it as Gopi's move to speak to his wife while he was absent. The lady must have told him that Gopi gave her the letter. He was angry and started shouting at Gopi when his parents came to support him. That made things worse and, in his rage, he made a move like he was going to hit Gopi. Seeing this Kochu Daveed jumped in to hold him back, which made him angrier. They both started to scuffle, and others interfered and separated them. The man started hurling obscenities at them and threatened to take revenge on Kochu Daveed soon. Theresa was upset with that and started crying. It took some time to console her.

The next day Kochu Daveed narrated this incident in his office and Mr. Nambiar said that he knew the local police inspector, who was his classmate. He would ask his help if needed. Kochu Daveed didn't want to make a big deal out of it. But Mr. Nambiar said, "You don't know much about these kinds of bullies. If they are not dealt with properly, they will create more problems. Let me deal with this." In the evening around 7.00, a police jeep stopped in front of their gate and a well-built police inspector walked into their common hall. He knocked on one of the doors and Gopi came out of the room. He told him to call everyone outside into the hall. Gopi ran around knocking on the doors and all the tenants gathered there. He then asked, "Who is Kochu Daveed?" Kochu Daveed stepped forward. He then asked, "Who was the one fighting with you?" Kochu Daveed pointed to the man in the third portion. "What is your name?" was his next question. "My name is Murugan, Sir" he replied. The Inspector said, "I understand that you have a wife and kid in another house, and you are in an illegal relationship with this lady here. Moreover, you have threatened to attack this Kochu Daveed who works with my friend. Now, you tell me how I should deal with you?" Murugan replied, "Please Sir, do not charge me with any case. I am willing to leave this place and I will not give any trouble to your friend. Please give me a week and I will move out of this place." The Inspector then said, "I will return after a week. Hope I don't see you here", then turning to Kochu Daveed he said, "Tell Nambiar that I had come here. If there are any more problems, do not hesitate to come to me." With that he returned to his jeep. All in the room except Murugan looked at Kochu Daveed with great respect. Theresa was happy to see that everything ended peacefully.

Within two days, Murugan and his partner vacated the house without saying goodbye to anyone. They must have not cleaned their house for a long time because, when they removed their cardboard boxes and other stuff, they could see cockroaches, centipedes, and scorpions scurrying out of their hiding places and getting into the neighbouring houses. In the next door, the little boy, Shankar's mother was putting her kids to sleep in the afternoon, when one of the scorpions fell on her from the ceiling. In a reflex action, she swiped the insect away from her body which went and fell on Shankar who was sleeping in the mat nearby. The stunned scorpion started stinging Shankar who jumped up and started crying. The scorpion clinging on to his trousers started to sting him all over his thighs. All the ladies came running out of their houses on hearing Shankar and his mother's cries. Gopi's father who had come home for lunch ran out and picked up Shankar. They could see that his legs started swelling where he was stung. He ran out with him, told Gopi to hold him and took them both to the local hospital in his cycle. Gopi's mother and Shankar's mother with her baby, ran behind them.

When Kochu Daveed returned home in the evening, he saw Theresa waiting near the door. She explained everything that happened in the afternoon and said that no one had returned from the hospital yet. They both anxiously waited outside for some news about Shankar. After about an hour they heard loud wailing noises coming from the street and then they saw them bringing the lifeless body of Shankar. Theresa fainted on seeing that and Kochu Daveed had to lift her up and take inside to revive her. She didn't come out of the house that day. She could hear the wailing cry of Shankar's mother the whole night. The next day they cremated the body and when they returned home, there was deadly silence all over. Theresa kept thinking of the lively boy and she couldn't stop her tears. She told Kochu Daveed that she will not be able to stay in that house anymore. He promised her that he would look for a new place immediately.

Chapter 13

The next house they moved in to was in Soliappan Street in Tondiarpet, nearer to his company. This house was owned by an old widow. When they were young, she and her husband had only one house in the centre of a nice plot of land. Her husband who foresaw a demand in rental properties while the city was growing towards the suburbs, demolished their house and built two rows of single bedroom houses with a common passage in the middle. They lived in the last house at the back and rented the other seven. Though he died young, his widow was able to meet all her expenses from the rental properties.

Kochu Daveed and Theresa moved to the first house on the right. Behind them was Ambrose and family, opposite to them was a bachelor artist/painter Antony D'Souza, behind him was Arumugam and Kannamma. The others were Krishnan, Parvathy and kids, two brothers of Pentecostal mission and a Telugu couple Ram and Sudha. Theresa soon found out that Mrs. Ambrose was a pious and friendly lady while the other ladies in the group Kannamma, Parvathy, and Sudha were very lively and boisterous. She got along well with everyone and she liked them all. But the one that caught her attention was the artist Antony. His surname clearly indicated that he was from an Anglo-Indian family, but he was dark with long hair, tall and well built and was always walking around wearing only a kind of shorts and Tee shirts. In the evenings he sits in the small yard in front and sings some English songs while strumming a guitar. When he opens the front door of his house you can see lots of books on one corner and his walls adorned with many of his paintings. His portion of the house was smaller than others and he doesn't have any other furniture than a table and chair and a cot in one corner. There was a big easel in the other corner with a canvas of half-finished painting.

Antony had a friendly nature and he talked to everyone. The other ladies warned Theresa to keep a distance from him because he was rumoured to be a womaniser. He had told them before of his many girl friends and how he goes on small trips with them and then dumps them. But she noticed that except for Mrs. Ambrose all the other ladies loved to flirt with him when they were alone. She tried her best to be with Mrs. Ambrose when she was alone in the house but felt drawn towards the other ladies when she heard them cracking jokes and laughing out loudly most of the time in the company of Antony.

One day while she was going to close her front door after seeing off Kochu Daveed to his office, she heard the door of Antony's house open and him calling her. He asked her, "Can I borrow some sugar? I was making coffee when I found that my sugar bottle is empty. I will return it in the evening after I do my grocery shopping." She smiled and brought him some sugar packed in a piece of paper. The next day at the same time he returned the borrowed sugar, which she refused to take back. The third day he opened the door as if on que when Kochu Daveed left and started talking to her. She always tried to make the conversations as short as possible. This became a daily habit and soon they were talking like old friends. Other ladies, Sudha, Parvathy, and Kannamma started joining them and hours seem to slip by in their bantering. The time spent with Mrs. Ambrose started to get less and less and soon her days started to revolve around Antony and evenings with her husband.

Kochu Daveed noticed that she was more into reading and was not chattering like before. He had two weeks of work in Vellore and he told her, "It is packing time again. We are going to Vellore for two weeks." She replied, "Vellore again! We already went there twice. There is nothing to see there. Why don't you go alone this time? I have good friends here. I will tell Kannamma to sleep in our house if I feel frightened in the night. I need to get used to your travel." Though he was surprised by her reply, he agreed with her logic. Yes, she needs to get used to staying alone and take care of the kids when we have start to expand our family, he thought. So, he said, "If you feel like that, then I am OK with it. I will try to come during the weekend." She replied, "Don't worry about me. I will be alright. Just give me the number of your office here. If there is any need, I will give them a call from the telephone booth."

Next day in the evening, when Kochu Daveed and Theresa were having their tea, they heard a knock on their door and when they opened it they saw Antony standing by the door. He smiled and gave them a package and said, "Sorry to disturb you. I did a rough sketch of you both and thought I would give it to you." Without waiting for any reply, he turned and left. They both opened it and saw a painting of a couple sitting in a beach, with the woman leaning on her partner and watching the sunset. The faces were not clear but the way their hair style was drawn it could be identified as Kochu Daveed and Theresa. He was not really impressed by the painting, but Theresa was very appreciative of it. She wanted it to be hung in their living room and Kochu Daveed was amused and agreed to it.

Kochu Daveed left for Vellore on Sunday evening, taking care to inform all his neighbours to take care of his wife. Kannamma's husband agreed to allow his wife to keep Theresa company in the night till he returned from Vellore. Theresa felt relieved that Kannamma was there with her in the night. Among all the ladies in that complex she was more comfortable with Kannamma because they had lots in common. She had wanted to talk freely to her for some time about her feelings for Antony but kept silent because she rarely got her alone. She started noticing that she felt happier in the company of Antony than of her husband. She had started comparing them both and found while her husband listens to all her chattering, Antony had really something to say about the books she read. They could have some real conversations and Antony always had some good observations, which she had not thought of before while reading. Everything about him made a favourable impression, his reading, painting, singing and music and his ease of talking with anyone. Compared to him, her husband looked dumb.

Right after Kochu Daveed left, Antony knocked at her door and gave her one more package. Though she wanted to invite him inside her house, she lost her courage at the last moment and just talked to him standing outside. She opened the package immediately and found her looking in to one of the most beautiful paintings of herself. She was so happy on seeing it that she didn't know what to say to him for a moment. She thought she had at last found her perfect partner who really appreciated her. Suddenly she came back to reality and thought how she could explain this painting to her husband. So, she returned the painting to him and said, "Please keep this with you. I don't want my husband asking questions about it. I will take it from you after some time." He accepted her logic and took it back and said, "I will place this in such a place where I can see it the first thing when I wake up and the last thing before I go to bed." She was so thrilled on hearing that. That night she told everything that happened to Kannamma, who was also as excited as her.

Their daily rendezvous went on without a hitch, with Kannamma as their look-out. They talked about all their interests, but Antony was not able to bring her to his room or go to her house. So, he suggested one day to go to the beach where they could talk more freely and plan their future. Theresa agreed on one condition that she would bring Kannamma with her. As planned, they met one afternoon in the Marina beach and with Kannamma sitting away from them, they decided to elope one day and start a new life in Goa, his hometown. That night while discussing it with Kannamma, who was supportive of their plan, she suddenly had a doubt whether he would stay loyal to her or leave her after some time. She expressed her fear to Kannamma, who had a solution for that too. She said, "Don't worry about that. Whenever we have some issues, we share our worries with one holy man here in Mylapore. On full moon nights, he goes to pray to Goddess Kali who enters his body and starts to speak to everyone. He looks very fearsome at that time. If anyone can go in front of him bravely and ask about their future, the Goddess will reply through him. We will go and meet him tomorrow and then on full moon night we will go and get the blessings of Goddess Kali."

The next day Kannamma took her to the holy man's hut in Mylapore. It was a small thatched hut with smell of camphor and incense sticks. In the dim light of the oil lamps in front of a large portrait of Goddess Kali, Theresa could see a middle-aged man in saffron clothes, listening with closed eyes to the words of one of the persons sitting on the ground in front of him. They both went and sat with the small group of people. After listening to the man in front of him, the holy man said something in low voice which they could not hear properly. The group sitting in front bowed before him and left. Kannamma took Theresa's hand and went forward. The holy man looked at them and Kannamma immediately bowed her head and with folded hands told him, "Swami, this is my friend, Theresa. She wants to know if the person she loves will take care of her their whole life." Swami closed his eyes for a moment and the said to them, "Will you be able to come here on the night of full moon at midnight?" Kannamma responded, "Yes Swami, we will come." The Swami then said, "Bring a gold bangle for Goddess Kali to wear. She will tell your future at that time." They both bowed down and left.

That Friday was full moon night. Since they both were not brave enough to go alone at midnight to Mylapore, they decided to take the help of Kannamma's husband. She told her husband that Theresa needed to see Swami to ask him when she would be a mother. She also told him that Theresa wanted to keep it a secret from her husband. Her husband agreed to drop them there in a rickshaw and wait for them till they finished their darshan (special appearance by a God or Goddess). On Friday night, they took a rickshaw and got down at the street corner leading to the Swami's place. Kannamma's husband stayed back with the rickshaw puller, while they both walked towards the hut of Swami. On nearing the hut, they saw a small crowd in front of the hut and in the centre was the Swami in glittering red saree, painted red lips and with a huge red sindhoor (traditional vermilion red color worn on the forehead by women) on his forehead. He was in a trance and was swaying back and forth. His hands were covered in the blood of the cockerel sacrificed during the pooja. Camphor was burning in different silver coloured plates in front of him. Suddenly he opened his eyes and looking directly at Theresa, took one piece of burning camphor in his bare hands, placed it on his blood-red tongue, closed his mouth and swallowed the fire. Then without taking eyes off her, he shouted in a feminine voice, "Theresa, go with the one you love, he will take care of you till the end." He closed his eyes again. Theresa handed over a gold bangle which was accepted by the assistant standing near the Goddess. The Goddess did not open her eyes for some time. Kannamma gestured to Theresa to return and they both bowed low and left.

Theresa couldn't sleep that night. The glowing face of Goddess Kali with blood-red lips kept appearing before her. The next day she didn't come out of her house. She was feeling feverish and so she just laid down in her bed. Kannamma came and helped her have some food. She explained to her that this fever is quite normal for someone getting a glimpse of the Goddess. She was already planning the elopement date on her behalf and Theresa felt that she was not in control of her life anymore. There was only one more week for Kochu Daveed to return. Kannamma wanted them to run away from there before he returned. But Theresa felt that something was not right. She remembered her mother saying that whenever she had to face a difficult situation and she didn't know what to decide, go and pray, talk to God, go through the Holy Bible, some solution is bound to appear. She wanted to do that, but Kannamma's presence was preventing her from doing it. So, she told Kannamma, "I am feeling better now. I will take a nap. Please go and finish your work at home. Come back in the evening, we will discuss again." When Kannamma left, she immediately went and knelt before the small altar in her house and started praying. When she took the Holy Bible to read, she naturally went to Psalm 91. She read Psalm 91 again and again and started to feel some peace. She understood one thing. Whether it was good or bad, she had to decide soon. Somehow, she was not so sure about the good intentions of Kannamma. But she trusted her God now and she knew that God will protect her from all dangers. With that peace of mind, she slept soundly till next morning.

Next day morning when she opened the front door, she saw Antony waiting for her. He said with a smile, "Kannamma told me everything. I am ready to go to Goa any time. I just need your date." "Wait till my husband's return. I don't want to leave without saying bye to him" she replied. Though he was confused about her present attitude, he did not say anything and went back to his room. When Kochu Daveed returned that weekend, he was pleasantly surprised to see her putting more efforts in serving his favorite dishes, which he thought was because she missed him these two weeks. Theresa did her best to leave a good impression on her husband. As the time to leave him was nearing, she realized that he was not all that bad. He had lots of good qualities, but he didn't have that dashing personality or the artistic talent of Antony. Then there was this nagging doubt that she might be pregnant. She knew that Kochu Daveed would be very happy to hear about that. But she didn't want to say anything now which might put a damper on her plans of elopement. And she didn't want to say anything yet to Antony also.

On Monday when Kochu Daveed went to office, Antony knocked on the door again to ask her about the future. She opened the door and they discussed in low voices about their next move. She agreed to leave the house the next day. They will first meet at the Marina Beach near Anna Samadhi in the morning. From there they will go to the railway station and travel to Goa. Antony would arrange the tickets. She just needs to come with whatever money and jewellery she had. He told her not to carry any suitcases, lest she be noticed by others. Though she was excited by the prospect of eloping with the love of her life, she maintained a calm posture in front of her husband and took extra care for all his needs. On Tuesday morning, after saying bye to her husband, she took whatever money she had saved and her jewellery in a small bag and left the house without locking it. She didn't want to inform even Kannamma about her plans. She walked till the main road and hailed an auto-rickshaw to go to the beach when she remembered that it was a Tuesday. On Tuesdays she and her husband regularly attend the novena of St. Antony of Padua in the St. Mary's Co-Cathedral. So, she thought it was best to start her new journey after praying to her favorite saint.

When she reached there, she saw that there was a long serpentine queue of people waiting for their turn to touch the feet of the miraculous statue of the saint, outside the church. She joined the queue in one end and started moving slowly towards the church. While standing and praying to the saint, she felt that she should discuss her pregnancy with Antony when she meets him in the beach. Once she made that decision, she felt a weight lifted from her heart. When her turn came, she knelt and then kissed the feet of her saint and with renewed vigour hailed another auto-rickshaw and went to Anna Samadhi.

Chapter 14

When the auto-rickshaw reached Anna Samadhi, she could see Antony sitting on the concrete bench impatiently. On seeing her a look of great relief was visible on his face. He said, "I thought you were not coming. I was waiting here for more than an hour." She replied, "On my way here, I dropped in to pray to St. Antony. Now I feel very liberated." He took hold of her hands and clasped it together and said, "You are going to be the most liberated woman in the world. We will live a life of full freedom, just the two of us. No one is going to separate us." His words and his first touch electrified her. She savoured in silence that divine moment. Then she said slowly, "I do have a confession to make. I think I am pregnant. I didn't tell this to my husband because I don't want him to shower his love on me and make it difficult to leave him. I don't know how you are going to take this too." His face darkened for a moment on hearing this but cleared very quickly. He said, "This does not change anything. Since this is just the beginning stage, we could easily abort it. I know doctors in Goa who can help us. We don't want any kids to spoil our happy life. We just need one another, no one comes in between us."

Her face turned pale on hearing this. Tears sprang from her eyes and she felt that someone had suddenly removed the veil that had blinded her for so long. She could see his bare soul and she did not like what she saw. When she regained her voice, she asked, "How could you say that? Abortion is same as killing. How could I kill my own child, and that too my first one?" He laughed pitilessly and said, "But that is not my child. Why should I bear the fruit of someone else? I wanted only you and you wanted a good and exciting life with me. I am giving you a release from your mundane life with your labourer husband. I don't need a child to destroy my artistic creativity. I chose you to be my muse because you looked different than others in your outlook and behaviour. But I think I was wrong." She started sobbing and in between her sobs she said, "I am a simple woman with very normal dreams and ambitions. I don't think I will rise to your level of artistic perfection. I fell for the mirage you created but your soul is just hollow and empty. You are just a selfish child." On hearing this he stomped away angrily, shouting abuses at her.

She sat down on the shade of the palm tree, completely exhausted and looking at the fading figure of him walking away. Suddenly she felt vulnerable and sad. She sat there and started crying. She thought of her husband and wondered how she had not realised so far that in her life with him till now, he had never said a harsh word to her. Thinking of him made her cry more. She wanted to put the blame on someone for her present condition. First, she wanted to blame her husband. If he had been a little more romantic, she would not have fallen for this charlatan. Then her anger turned towards Antony who tried to take advantage of her inexperience in the world. He awakened her long-lost romanticism and spirit of adventure. Now she knew she would not go back to her normal self. Then she started to blame her parents who brought her up like a princess and then abandoned her to a mediocre life. In between she also wanted to kill Kannamma for encouraging her in this affair. Finally, she decided that she was to blame for everything that happened. She should not have tried to bring to life the romantic scenes from her old English novels.

She didn't know what to do now. She did know how long she had been sitting there. For a moment she considered walking towards the sea and keep walking until she drowned. She instinctively knew that it must be how her cousin died in the sea long time ago. Shouldn't she just go and meet her cousin? Then she remembered that she might be pregnant, and the love of her life just left her because she dared to save her child. She is not going to kill her child. How about going back to her parents? Will they understand and support her? Her parents might support her, but they are dependant on her brother, who would not agree to add on one more burden. She had no place to go and that thought made her cry again. The sun was going to set soon, and she knew that her husband must be searching for her.

In the meantime, Kochu Daveed was running around looking for Theresa. No one knew where she had gone. When he returned home in the evening, the door was left unlocked and she was no where to be found. First, he checked with her friends and even her close friend Kannamma was totally unaware of her whereabouts. Everyone from the complex including Antony, started looking for her. In the evening, the owner of the small sweet shop in front of the house came and told them that his little son had seen her going out in the morning. The only thing he noticed about her was she was wearing a blue colored saree and holding a rosary in her hands. When it started to get dark, they decided to inform the police about the missing woman. Mr. Nambiar's friend was still the Inspector in that police station. So, he took things very seriously and informed all the police stations to look out for a Malayali woman in blue-colored saree. By midnight they received a message from the beach police station that they found a woman lying unconscious near Anna Samadhi and admitted her to the General Hospital. She was wearing a blue saree.

When Kochu Daveed reached the hospital, she was still unconscious. She was in the general ward and the doctors were giving her intra venous saline. He identified her as his wife Theresa and the policemen who brought her in gave him her small handbag, which had some money in it. The doctors told him that she was very weak, and lack of food must have made her unconscious. The policemen asked him if he knew why she was there in the beach. He told them the truth that he returned home from work in the evening and found their house empty and unlocked. He had no knowledge of what had happened from the time he left for work till evening. After the policemen left, he pulled aside a stool and sat near his wife's bed. The duty nurse kept coming every half hour to check on her. While sitting there he was thinking about the story she had told earlier about how her dead cousin had come and invited her to go to the sea with her. He wondered whether it happened again. He used to believe in ghosts when he was a kid and later stopped thinking about it when he grew up. But suddenly he felt very afraid.

By early morning, she showed signs of waking up and so he called the nurse to check. When the nurse was checking her pulse, Theresa opened her eyes and looked around bewildered. She had no idea of where she was at that time. The last she remembered was thinking that it was getting dark and she was still sitting near the Anna Samadhi. She looked around and her eyes rested on her husband who was anxiously staring at her. She felt weak and managed to give a faint smile. Then she closed her eyes again. Everything that happened so far went through her mind and she did not have the courage to look at the face of her husband. She didn't know what to say. With closed eyes she started to pray to her favorite St. Antony. "I know I committed a big mistake, but please help me St. Antony. If I am alive, I will come and attend your novena every Tuesday. Please help me." She kept praying repeatedly. She knew she couldn't pretend like she was sleeping for long. After some time, she opened her eyes and looked at Kochu Daveed with tears welling in her eyes. She was shedding tears of remorse, but he mistook that as an apology for causing him grief and pain. He too started crying and he controlled himself and said, "Don't worry. You are safe now. Your cousin will not come and take you again. It is the answer to my prayers to God and St. Antony that you came back to me safe and sound. I will never miss a novena for St. Antony in my life."

She was going to reply when they saw the doctor coming towards them. He was smiling at them and they both felt reassured by his smile. "I am here to give you both good news" he started saying. He then turned to Kochu Daveed and said, "Your wife is pregnant. She is anaemic and so we had to do some tests. It shows positive for the pregnancy tests. Congratulations!" Then he continued, "We will discharge her today morning. Just give her good food and let her regain her weight." With that he left. She suddenly saw a way out of this mess she had created. She looked at her husband who was looking very happily surprised. She said, "If you will not get mad at me, I want to tell you something." He nodded his head smiling, so she continued, "I felt that I may be pregnant. I thought I would surprise you with a test report. That was the reason I went out yesterday without informing you." He looked more surprised and she continued, "I thought I will go and pray to St. Antony first and then go to a clinic to do the test. The auto-rickshaw driver was taking me through the beach road, when I felt that I should get down there. I remember walking towards the beach and then I don't remember anything." He clasped her hands tightly and said, "God has protected you from the evil spirits. I think we should go and get blessings from the priest."

She then remembered her visit to the holy man's house with Kannamma and her husband. She didn't want him to know about that from them. So, she said, "Last week I had gone with Kannamma and her husband to visit a holy man through whom Goddess Kali speaks. He also told that I will be pregnant soon." Hearing this her husband said, "Why do you go to such places. That holy man must be dealing with evil spirits. Something from there must have followed you and was trying to take your life. You should stop your friendship with Kannamma. I don't like her." With melancholic eyes she said, "I don't think I will like to stay in that house anymore. Why can't we go back to Kochi for some time?" He agreed to that plan. He said he will try to get a week's leave and take her back to his parent's house.

When she was discharged from the hospital, they returned home and found that Kannamma and her husband were waiting for them with food prepared at their home. Though Kochu Daveed didn't want to mingle with them, on Theresa's insistence he politely accepted their hospitality and thanked them for it. All other neighbours also visited them except Antony. His house was locked from outside. In between the buzz of all the people in the house, Theresa managed to tell Kannamma to come alone the next day, so that she can tell her what happened. Kochu Daveed did not leave her side the whole day and they had a well-needed sleep that night. Next day he went to his office to ask for a week's vacation, so that he could leave his pregnant wife back at her home. Kannamma came immediately after he left. Theresa told her what happened and came to know from her that Antony had gone to some far away place to concentrate on his painting. Theresa felt relieved that she could share her story to at least one person who would not judge her. She also told her about their plans to stay in Kochi for some time. Kannamma assured her that her secret will not be revealed to anyone. Though she was disappointed that the love story in which she played an important part did not end well, she decided to be true to her friend. She also sensed that Kochu Daveed did not like her very much, so, she returned home as soon as she got to know the whole story.

Kochu Daveed returned home in the afternoon in a happy mood. He was able to get a week's leave from his work. So, on the way home he went and booked two tickets for the next day's train to Kochi. Everything went well and when they got down in front of their home in Kochi. His parents were surprised to see them there. When they heard from Kochu Daveed that Theresa was pregnant, they were filled with happiness and promised him that she would be taken care of very well. He did not tell them any other details of their recent adventure.

Kochu Daveed's parents also had some good news to share with them. They were in the process of writing him a letter regarding a marriage proposal for his youngest sister. The boy runs his own business in Cherthala, a small town near Alappuzha. He and his married elder brother lived in a comfortable house there that they owned. The brother had no kids of their own. One of his uncles who was a friend of Mariamma's brother had brought them this proposal. They thought it was a good one and wanted to ask Kochu Daveed his opinion. He told them that, since he had only one week's vacation, he was planning to visit Theresa's parents the next day. On the way there he would go and meet this guy and then decide what to do.

The next day they went to Alappuzha and surprised everyone there also. They were given a warm welcome and they stayed a night there. On their return they met the boy, Avarachan, in his small store, liked the way he was handling everything and on reaching home informed his parents about his approval of the guy his parents had found for his sister. In the evening after they had a family prayer and supper, they gathered around in the verandah to discuss further about the wedding. Pathro then told them what he had discussed while meeting the boy's elder brother. He said,

"The elder brother, Paulose, has his own store in another town but they all live together in one house. They don't have any kids and they are not planning to adopt one too. He had two conditions for the marriage. The first one was that the girl should agree to live with them in that house. They are not supposed to move out. The second one was about the dowry to be given. They are not asking for any money, but they would like to have at least enough gold on the neck and hands of the bride. He said that his wife has around 200 grams of gold. We should be able to match that."

Kochu Daveed asked, "How much do we have with us now?" His mother replied, "I have saved around 100 grams with me." Then he replied, "Let me see if I can get some loan from the bank. I am sure that I can manage money for 50 grams of gold." Then Theresa said, "I will give 50 grams from my gold. She is my sister too. We don't want to drop this proposal because of shortage of gold." Everyone was happy on hearing that. Pathro then said, "I will take care of the wedding expenses. I will inform Paulose tomorrow itself and proceed with fixing the wedding date." They all went to sleep with satisfaction that they had made a good decision. Theresa was more thankful to God that she was able to create a good impression in front of her husband and his family. She wanted to leave behind whatever happened due to her immature behaviour and start a new life with her husband. Her only prayer was that he does not find out about her brief fling with Antony.

The meeting with Pathro and Paulose went well and they decided on a wedding date two months later. Kochu Daveed returned to Madras, leaving behind Theresa, promising to come at least a week before the wedding. He also promised her that he would take her back to Madras after the wedding, but it would be to a better house.

Chapter 15

Kochu Daveed was busy with his work for the first few days after reaching Madras. He left home early in the morning and returned late at night. He had already informed his superiors about the impending marriage of his sister and he was also looking into raising the required amount for the gold. Only on the weekend did Kannamma get a chance to ask him about Theresa. He explained to her that she would be staying with her parents for some time and return to Madras only after the wedding of his sister. On Sunday, she and her husband invited him for lunch, which he accepted graciously. Mr. & Mrs. Ambrose also started sending him parcels of food whenever he was home alone in the evenings. He noticed that Antony was no longer living in the house in front of him. On enquiry he found out that he had vacated the house while they were in Kochi.

On the next weekend he was invited again for lunch by Kannamma and her husband. While having lunch, he casually told them that he knew about their visit to their Godman along with Theresa. The color drained off from the face of Kannamma and she blurted out, "Did she say everything to you?" Kochu Daveed smiled and said, "Yes, she did. She also told me that you are the one who wanted to take her there." On hearing this Kannamma started crying and said, "Sorry for all the trouble. She was a good lady and my best friend. I wanted her to have a happy life and so I helped her in whatever way I could. Please do not blame me for all that had happened." Kochu Daveed got nervous on seeing her crying. He told her not to worry and he finished his lunch quickly and left. On reaching home he was thinking that there was more to what happened to Theresa and Kannamma knew everything. He had to find out all that he could. Kannamma looked really terrified in front of him today. She must surely know more than she let her husband know. Her husband was equally baffled by the tears of Kannamma.

That night when he wrote a letter to Theresa, he mentioned about the crying incident at Kannamma's house and his suspicion that she was covering up something, which even her husband doesn't know. The whole of next week he did not see Kannamma. Looked like she was hiding from him. Her husband did talk to him sometimes, just casual talk. Only Mr. Ambrose was keeping him company when he was alone in his house. He seemed to be a very decent and God-fearing man. Normally their talks turned to Bible and he was very eloquent on every chapter of the Holy book. Psalms was his favorite section and he made Kochu Daveed read Psalm 91 daily. His next favorite one was Psalm 23. Kochu Daveed started enjoying his daily discourses with Mr. Ambrose and his interest in learning more about the Holy Bible got ignited again after a long time. It looked like it was God's way of preparing him to face one of the worst crises in his life.

Next week he received a reply from Theresa and on reading it he felt that his whole life has come crashing down around him. He held that letter and sat there too stunned to move. Tears flowed from his eyes as he went through that letter again. Theresa had confessed to all that had happened in the fear that he would somehow get to know everything from Kannamma. She wrote how she was feeling disconnected with him and how Antony showed up like a dream come true to her immature mind. He felt a deep pain like a sword in his heart when he read about how she decided to elope with her lover. He was undecided on what to feel when he read about her going to pray at St. Antony's Chapel and how she thought that the Saint had rescued her from the clutches of evil. He didn't know if he was supposed to be relieved that the Saint saved her or get angry at God for making him suffer like this. When Mr. Ambrose knocked on the door for his daily visit, he found Kochu Daveed sitting in the dark, holding a letter in his hand. When the light was put on, he could see that he was crying, and he knew that something very bad had happened. So, he said, "Looks like you are having a bad day. If you want to be alone with your thoughts, I will go back. But if you think you can share with me your sorrows, I will sit here and lighten your burden." Kochu Daveed replied, "Let me wash my face and come. If I sit here alone for any more time, I will have a mental breakdown. Please stay with me for some time. I really

don't know if I want to unburden myself on you." He went to
wash his face and when he returned, he found that Mr. Ambrose
had gone back to his house. He was wondering if he should go
there and call him, when Kochu Daveed returned. He told him, "I
went back to tell my wife to prepare tea for both of us. She will
be back soon." They both sat on the chairs and was silent for some
time. Then Kochu Daveed started to talk.

"I received a letter from my wife, Theresa, today. I don't know
how to say it. I think no husband should be getting a letter like
this. She confessed to an affair with our neighbour, Antony. The
part that hurt me most was her decision to leave me and start a
life with him. She says that St. Antony intervened and saved her.
But I don't know if I could believe her anymore and count this as
a blessing. You have more knowledge than me in religious
matter. Do you think it was good for God to play with my life
like this? In my life so far, I have trusted God so much that I had
the same kind of trust in all human beings. Now, with this
incident, I am not only losing trust in humankind, but also in
God."

Mr. Ambrose replied, "I am sorry to hear about your
misfortune. My wife did give me a hint that something was
happening between Antony and the other ladies in this
compound. We didn't think that your wife would be involved in
this. We tried to keep to ourselves and not interfere in other's
life. But it was shocking to hear from you about this." Kochu
Daveed then said, "My wife confessed her mistake only because
she was afraid that I would know the truth from Kannamma. As
a punishment for her mistake, she is willing to separate from me
and go live with her parents. But she wants to stay with me till
the wedding of my sister. I think I agree with her decision."

"Please don't take any hasty decisions at the heat of the
moment" Mr. Ambrose said. "I understand your anger and it is
justified. Before taking any decisions, why don't you talk to her
first? As human beings, we make mistakes, but we become better
human beings only when we forgive and forget. And we can't

blame God for the mistakes that we make. God gave us enough intelligence to distinguish between right and wrong." "So, what should I do now?" Kochu Daveed asked. "You will be going back within a month for your sister's wedding. For now, write a letter asking her to wait till the wedding functions are over and after that you both can discuss and come to an agreement. But till that time, don't stop your prayers, be as calm as possible and leave everything in God's hands." Mr. Ambrose replied.

The days seemed to go very slowly for Kochu Daveed. Mr. Ambrose visited him daily in the evening and gave him calm reassurance. By the time he was ready to go back, he was able to raise enough money for the gold. At last the day arrived for him to return to Kochi. He dreaded meeting Theresa and talking to her. He didn't want anyone in the house to know anything. When he reached home, he tried his best to act normally in front of others. Even Theresa seemed to act like nothing happened between them. In the night when everyone retired to their rooms, after closing the door to their room, Theresa looked at him and said, "I am really sorry for hurting you. It was my mistake that I did not tell you everything while I was in the hospital. I didn't have the courage to openly tell about my affair. I know I am in the wrong and you have every right to punish me for that. After this wedding, I will go away from your life and will not bother you again. Please do not let others know about my foolishness." Tears were flowing down her eyes by the time she finished talking. Kochu Daveed was also crying and he said, "We can talk about this later. Let us finish our duty first."

The next day, they went shopping for gold and wedding outfits for everyone. In the evening, Theresa gave them some of her gold which she had promised earlier. Everyone got so busy with the preparations that both Kochu Daveed and Theresa did not have the energy and strength to discuss about their future. The wedding and the party after that went very well. After the customary stay of three days, the bride and groom returned to the groom's house. Only four people remained in the house and Kochu Daveed had only three more days before returning to Madras. He told his parents that Theresa wanted to stay for some days with her parents before coming to Madras. So, with their permission they left for Alappuzha the next day. On their way they stopped at the famous Church of St. Sebastian in Arthungal and went in to pray. Since it was a weekday, and, afternoon time, no one was there in the church. After praying for some time, Theresa said to him, "I think this is going to be our last trip together. Before I go, I want you to understand that I have always loved and respected you. You have a good heart and God will always protect the ones with good heart. I was blinded by my ignorance and I fell for a charlatan. I realised it only at the last moment. I assure you in front of our God and saviour, that though I had fallen for another man, I had not given him my body or my soul. My mind did play some tricks on me. But now I am back to my senses. If you can, please forgive me. That is all I ask from you."

Kochu Daveed bowed his head and listened to all she said. He then closed his eyes and prayed to God to show him the right way. After the prayer he opened his eyes and said, "When I first read your letter of confession, I had decided never to see your face again. It was Mr. Ambrose who talked to me for a long time and made me see the facts from a different view. If the feelings of repentance in you are true, then I am willing to forgive and forget what you have done. But I need an assurance from you, in front of our God and all his saints, that you would not commit this act again in our life." Tears of joy flowed from Theresa's eyes and for a moment she was not able to say anything. She then said, "I promise you, in front of our God and all the saints, that I will not commit such an act against you in our lifetime together." They both held each others' hands tightly as if confirming their togetherness again. They said a prayer of gratitude for bringing them together again and with great relief in their heart, went out and continued their journey to her parents' house.

Theresa's youngest brother offered to bring her back to Madras after one month and meanwhile, Kochu Daveed would find a better house for them to live. As per the custom, Theresa would go back to her parent's house on her seventh month of pregnancy, for the first childbirth. Everyone agreed to that and Kochu Daveed returned to Kochi to travel back to Madras.

On reaching Madras, the first thing Kochu Daveed did was to meet Mr. and Mrs. Ambrose and share with them all the things that happened in Kochi. They both were happy to see that the couple had come together. They decided to help him find a better house for them to live. Two blocks away they were able to find a house in Thandavaraya Street which was a better neighbourhood. This complex had five houses in a row but with enough space for kids to run around. The landlord lived in the last house and the other renters were all young families with small kids. Kochu Daveed liked the house and the neighbours and he booked the house for the next month by paying the initial deposit.

Chapter 16

Theresa and her brother reached Madras after a month and they both liked the new house and its neighbours. Their house was the second one from the street. In the first one lived a Jain family from Rajasthan with five kids, behind them lived a Hindu family from Andhra Pradesh with two small daughters. In the fourth house lived a Tamil couple with one son. Theresa's brother stayed with them for a month and then went back home. After he left both Kochu Daveed and Theresa did their best to avoid any kind of confrontation, which might lead to reopening any old wounds. They had monthly check-ups with a Gynaecologist and as planned earlier they returned to Kochi before the starting of seventh month to get ready for the customary visit to her parent's house.

Theresa's eldest brother and sister-in-law came to Kochi to take her to her parents' house. She gave birth to a baby boy and everyone was very happy on receiving him as God's gift. A month after the baptism of the boy, Theresa's mother collapsed and was admitted to the hospital from where she returned only as a dead body after a week. While returning to Madras after the funeral, Theresa was thinking about her father, who was behaving like he had lost his will to live after her mother's death. She knew that she will have to come back again for her father soon. As she had expected, she received a telegram from her brother asking them to come immediately to see her father who was seriously ill in the hospital. So, within six months of losing her mother, she lost her father too. She grieved for them for some time and then recovered enough to take care of her small son and her husband.

After about three months from the day her father died, she received a letter from her youngest brother, asking her if he can come and stay with her for some time. He also wanted to look for some job in Madras. Theresa was excited to have him in her house, though Kochu Daveed thought that he would become a burden for them. Theresa was happy that her wayward brother was at last taking life seriously and wanted to do some work and become a responsible person. On her insistence, Kochu Daveed agreed to take his brother-in-law with him when went for his next work outside the state. He kept his word when he got a big contract work at JIPMER hospital in Pondicherry. They all went together and stayed in a rental house for four months till the work was over. It was during that time that they came to know the real reason her brother left his house. Their father, before his death, had willed all his property to his eldest son, because he was the one who was taking care of all the expenses in the house. He did put in a clause that the eldest son should give appropriate share to his brothers if he plans to sell the property. For the first two months after their father's death things seemed to be getting back to normal. The two youngest unmarried brothers came home only during the night to sleep. Otherwise they were outside, doing their own things, mostly playing cards with their friends and making some money out of it. They both were good card players.

But one day, their eldest brother called them aside and said, "I am finding it difficult to manage all expenses with my present job. I have an offer from a rubber plantation in Punalur as the estate manager. I am planning to move there with my family. You two can stay here and take care of the property till we can find some one to buy it." The thought of selling their ancestral house was not acceptable to them, but they had no power to stop it because everything was in the elder brother's name. Within two weeks the family moved to Punalur leaving them both in charge of the house. And within one week of that, prospective buyers started showing up at their house. The sale was fixed in no time and one day their elder brother came home in the evening and gave each of them two thousand five hundred rupees and said that that was their share from the sale of their house. When they argued that the house itself is worth more than that, he presented them with the medical bills of both their father and mother and the other expenses he had to bear for all of them. He had reduced those expenses from the amount he got for the property and dividing equally, that was the amount he gave them. When they asked about the share for the second brother living in Bangalore and the sisters, he just gave the same amount for the brother only. "We have given enough gold for the girls, so they don't deserve anything from this" he said and ended the discussion there.

Both Kochu Daveed and Theresa were very upset on hearing this from her brother. Though they didn't expect anything from her elder brother, they did not like the way he treated his siblings. Theresa wrote a very long letter to her brother accusing him of taking advantage of a dying father and forcing him to will everything to him. In return she got a letter explaining all the difficulties he faced while taking care of the sick parents and how he was in huge debt because of that. The sale of the property did not bring him any profit but was used up to clear all his debts. Though she wanted to send a reply to him calling out his bluff, Kochu Daveed told her not to do so. He told her to let it go and avoid any more future communication with her elder brother. That was the end of one relationship.

After the work at Pondicherry was over, they returned to Madras. Theresa's bother decided to go back to Alappuzha with the money he earned and rented out a small house for him to stay and try to start a card game club along with that. He said that if he was able to arrange a small place of gathering for his friends to play cards and charge a small fee for using that place, he would be able to earn a living out of that. Kochu Daveed and Theresa agreed to let him do what he is passionate about and so he left them.

Their life started to flow peacefully. Soon she was pregnant with her second child and then gave birth to a baby girl. This time they stayed in Kochi at Kochu Daveed's house and had a wonderful time there. His parents liked the noise and commotion made by the kids and they commented that the house had become lively after a long time. They all went back to Madras after the baptism of the child. A few months after that they received a telegram from Kochi saying that his father had died and to come home immediately. This was such a shock for him as he knew that his father was looking healthy when they last saw him. Since it was difficult to travel in unreserved compartment in the train with small kids and the small one being sick, Kochu Daveed decided to go alone to Kochi. On reaching there he learnt how his father died.

Pathro had gone to attend his daily mass at the church early in the morning. The guy sitting near him in the church had seen him bend and touch his forehead to the ground during the final blessing. But he did not get up even when everyone started to leave the church. So, he shook him slowly to make him get up when he rolled over and fell. Everyone immediately gathered around and tried to wake him up, but he was already dead. The parish priest came and said prayers for his soul. One of the parishioner's fetched a doctor who confirmed his death. Then they sent another parishioner to his house to inform the family.

After the funeral, Kochu Daveed wanted to take his mother to Madras, but she decided to stay there at Kochi. So, he entrusted his cousin, Stephan, who lived nearby to take care of her. Stephan told him that he would send his wife and one of his daughters to keep her company during the night. Within a month of reaching Madras he received another telegram from Stephan asking him to come immediately. Fearing the worse and thinking that something happened to his mother, he took an emergency leave from the office and went back. When he reached there, he found his mother to be well and good but the look on her face was painful. He asked the reason for her pained look and Stephan explained it to him.

Two days back, Chandy, the brother of his eldest brother-in-law, had come there with some workers to pick the coconuts from their plot surrounding the house. When Stephan and Kochu Daveed's mother asked him why he is taking the coconuts from their property, he waved a piece of paper in their face and told them that this property belongs to his brother now. He had papers to prove that Pathro had willed the whole property and the house to his eldest son-in-law. When he heard that, Stephan got mad and went in to his house and came back with a large sickle and brandishing that in the air shouted at them, "If anyone dared to pick the coconuts from this property, I will cut off the foot that steps on this soil. This is Kochu Daveed's property and no one should enter it unless he comes and makes a decision." Seeing his rage, everyone left immediately.

Kochu Daveed then asked his mother, "How could father have done this to me?" His mother replied, "Son, I don't think your father would have done this. Do you remember Chandy coming here daily and drinking with your father?" He replied, "Yes, that was the main reason I ran away from home." Then his mother said, "I think that cunning Chandy must have got your father to sign some papers when he was drunk. That is why he is coming now with this claim after your father is dead. We will go and meet one of your father's cousin who is a lawyer. He might be able to help us." They went and met Advocate Joseph, who gladly agreed to help them. He assured them that, even if his brother-in-law had legitimate papers with him, he will get back the property to Kochu Daveed. He immediately applied for an injunction order which banned anyone else other than Kochu Daveed and his mother from enjoying the use of their property. They could not sell it until the court proceedings were over. He returned to Madras after settling that issue and leaving Stephan to protect his mother and his property.

The court case dragged on for two years and finally was settled in favour of Kochu Daveed. Since his eldest sister was legally entitled to one-sixth of the property, the court ordered him to pay her an amount equivalent to that. But Kochu Daveed did not have that much money to give. So, he gave her one-sixth of the property from one corner of the land. Stephan worked hard for this case, going to the court regularly for all the hearings in place of Kochu Daveed and following up with the advocate. During this time, his business suffered a setback and he had some great losses. To clear his debts, he had to sell his property and move to a rental place. In those days, rentals were not common in the Kochi area. People normally lease a house for a year and pay a lump sum amount, which was returned when the lease time was over. The owner of the house can invest the money in anything and earn profits from it. He needs to give only the original amount back. When Kochu Daveed heard about the difficulties of Stephan, he wrote to him asking him to move in with his mother. But being a man of self-respect, Stephan refused to accept his free accommodation. So, Kochu Daveed agreed to accept some lease amount and allowed Stephan and family to move to his parents' house. His mother needed only one bedroom and a kitchen. Stephan and family moved into the other rooms. They built a temporary kitchen behind the house with thatched coconut leaves and started using that instead.

This arrangement was beneficial to both the families. Kochu Daveed was able to stop worrying about his mother being lonely and at the same time Stephan could relax and concentrate on bringing his business back without worrying about moving houses every year. Kochu Daveed's sisters were not very happy about this arrangement. They thought that it hindered their freedom while coming to visit their mother. But Kochu Daveed was firm in his decision. He told them that he would reconsider his decision if one of his sisters were ready to take care of his aging mother. But they were not ready for that. So, the matter was decided with an uneasy truce between the brother and sisters.

In the meantime, Theresa gave birth to a third child, a boy. Their life began to move peacefully, with the older kids starting school and Theresa busy with the household duties and kids. Kochu Daveed was promoted to the position of Assistant Engineer and he was quite proud of his achievement. In the new position there were more responsibilities. He was able to handle all the technical aspects very well. But he struggled when it came to writing long reports. Theresa would help him with that when he returned from a long contract work outside the state. He would write everything in Malayalam before reaching home and Theresa would translate it to English which he would submit to the head office the next day.

They thought that their life was going smoothly. Their only worry was his aging mother. With Stephan and family living in the same house, they knew she would be taken care of. Then Theresa started to feel little weak in the evenings. They thought that she might be lacking in some vitamins. Their family doctor prescribed some for her. But she still felt too tired by the time she went to bed at night. She started to feel dizzy when getting up from the chair. The doctor found that her blood pressure was rising and so he wanted to monitor her for a week before prescribing some medicines. He sent her for complete blood work and the results came with a shocking news that her kidneys are losing their function. Her family physician referred her to a Nephrologist who confirmed that she had a hereditary disease called Polycystic kidneys. Both her kidneys were affected, and they needed to take immediate action to slow down the kidney failure.

Chapter 17

The Nephrologist at the Government Royapettah Hospital, after examining the X-Ray and the scan reports confirmed that Theresa had polycystic kidneys. They asked her if anyone in her family had a history of kidney diseases. She said that her mother died of kidney-related issues, but she does not know if she had polycystic kidneys. The doctor explained that this is a genetic disorder in which the renal tubules become structurally abnormal leading to growth of multiple cysts within the kidneys. When the cysts enlarge, they crush the adjacent tubules rendering them non-functional. There is currently no cure for polycystic kidney disease, and it is not possible to stop the cysts forming in the kidneys. The doctor suggested that he could perform a surgery to remove some of the larger cysts, but that would not completely cure her. She will surely have a kidney failure and in that case, she will need a kidney transplant or go for dialysis.

Kochu Daveed decided to take the risk and agreed for a surgery. He wrote to his mother about Theresa and her surgery. She wrote back saying that Stephan agreed to send his wife and one of his daughters to help him take care of the kids while Theresa was in the hospital. Kochu Daveed was so thankful to Stephan and believed that God was back again to help him in his time of need. So, he went ahead and fixed a date for the surgery. Within a week, Stephan's wife Marykutty and her daughter Susan arrived in Madras. Marykutty stayed with Theresa in the hospital and Susan took care of the kids and the cooking.

The surgery was successful, and she was discharged after two weeks. The doctor told her to take complete rest for at least a month. Marykutty and Susan took care of everything in the house and after a month when Theresa was able to move around slowly, Marykutty decided to go back home, leaving Susan there to help them. Theresa felt very bored from sitting idle in one place and letting Susan do all the work. So, she started to do some light duties around the house, when Kochu Daveed left for work. One day she was trying to lift the vessel with cooked rice to drain the water from it, when she felt pain in her sides. Susan panicked and with the help of neighbours, took Theresa to the nearby private hospital. It was a small hospital with around twenty beds in it. The doctor admitted her there and Kochu Daveed reached there when one of the neighbours informed his office. He was upset with Susan for allowing Theresa to do such work at home. But Theresa took the blame on herself and felt sorry for him. They discharged her after two days with strict orders not to lift any heavy objects.

Even though the surgery did remove the big cysts in her kidney, other smaller ones started to grow bigger and her kidney functions started to reduce again. The constant pain, frequent visits to the hospital and the helplessness one feels when one can't do anything by oneself, made Theresa more irritable day by day. She started to think that she was a burden in the life of her husband and children. Susan tried her best to keep the house running and at the same time kept an eye on Theresa, and made sure she didn't exert herself. Theresa started to suspect that Kochu Daveed was having an affair with Susan because he was discussing everything concerning the house with Susan only. One day they had an argument when Theresa told him about her suspicion. He wanted to burst out in anger on hearing that but controlled himself with the thought that she was doing this only because she was sick. A sick body might be affecting her mind too. Susan did not have that magnanimity of heart. She broke down in tears on hearing that and insisted that she be sent back home to Kochi. She was already having her hands full with taking care of the kids and the house. She was not going to put up with any unnecessary rumours regarding an affair with a person whom she called 'Achayan' (Elder brother). Kochu Daveed told her to wait for some more time. He told her that he would send them all to Kochi by the end of March, when the school closes for summer. Susan agreed to that.

Kochu Daveed and Theresa had some good and peaceful discussion regarding their future. They decided to return to their hometown Kochi when the school closed for summer. For the next academic year, the kids would study in a good school in Kochi. Theresa could stay home and get some rest in a good peaceful atmosphere. Kochu Daveed's mother and Stephan's family would be there to help her out. He himself would stay back in Madras and within one year try to get transferred to the Kerala branch of Indian Oxygen Ltd. Her treatment could be followed up by the doctors referred by her Nephrologist. They discussed this plan with their family doctor and the kidney specialist too. Everyone thought that it was a good for Theresa's health.

They moved to Kochi as per their plan. The kids were sad to leave their friends in Madras, but they were willing to settle in Kochi and find new friends for the sake of their mother's health. Kochu Daveed returned to Madras after letting them settle in Kochi. He decided to keep staying in the same rental house for a year more, just in case Theresa decided to come back. The fresh air and change in the living conditions did improve the health of Theresa for some time. Her only problem was the lack of privacy in the house with two families living together. Stephan's family did their best to help her out. With Kochu Daveed out in Madras, Theresa became good friends with Susan and her younger sisters.

By the mid-October, Theresa started to get sick again. The doctors in Kochi told her to contact her Nephrologist in Madras. When Kochu Daveed informed the Nephrologist of the symptoms shown by Theresa, the doctor told him to either bring her back immediately and admit her in the hospital or if she was too weak to travel, to get her admitted to a good hospital in Kochi and start dialysis. Theresa decided to go back to her own Nephrologist and so leaving the kids behind with their grandmother, she along with Susan and one of her brothers, Jacob, went to Madras. On reaching there, she was taken to the hospital directly and they hooked her up on to the dialysis machine.

Initially they did dialysis three times a week. Since travelling to and from the house was difficult, they admitted her in the general ward and continued with the dialysis. Susan was there with her most of the time. Though she was getting better after dialysis, she felt very weak and tired after each session. By December her condition started to deteriorate and she began to drift in and out of consciousness. Whenever she woke up from her unconscious state, she started to ask about her kids. So Kochu Daveed decided to send Jacob back to Kochi and bring their kids to Madras. Jacob did as he was told to when the kids reached the hospital, Theresa was unconscious again. The kids were very upset and started crying and calling her. She did move her hands on hearing the cries of her children, but she didn't open her eyes. The doctor came and said that she is probably going into a coma state. She might come back, but it was in the hands of the Almighty.

Kochu Daveed sent back the kids with Jacob after buying them food and he stayed back in the hospital with Susan. Around midnight, he was sitting in the bench outside the ward and Susan was sitting beside Theresa's bed with her head on the side bar of the bed, when they both heard Theresa saying something loudly. Kochu Daveed ran inside and saw that Susan was holding Theresa's left hand which was flaying around and trying to calm her down. Theresa was calling out her children's names and crying and Susan was also crying and saying, "Don't worry, Chechi! I will take care of them." Kochu Daveed held on to her right hand and felt that Theresa was getting calm and stopped flaying her hands. Slowly they could feel all her movements stopping. He ran out immediately and called the duty nurse who came running with the resident doctor. She was dead by the time they reached her. Kochu Daveed slumped by the bedside and started crying. Susan too was wailing loudly. Kochu Daveed stopped crying when the doctor asked him to proceed with the formalities of releasing the body from the hospital. He did everything mechanically and when all the formalities were completed, he took Theresa's body to their rental house in an ambulance.

Jacob and the children were woken up by the neighbours when the body was brought home. The kids did not understand at first what was happening. But they broke down when they saw them carrying in the body of their mother. As the night turned to daylight, everyone started to ask Kochu Daveed about the funeral arrangements. He said that he had sent telegrams to all his and her close relatives in Kerala and was expecting some of them to come. So, they decided to wait for one more day and take the body to the cemetery the next day morning. Theresa's brother in Bangalore and the youngest one from Alappuzha reached that night itself. Kochu Daveed's elder sister along with her son-in-law also reached the next day morning. But Theresa's eldest brother didn't come and when contacted later said that he got confused about the place of the funeral and went to Kochi to attend it.

Kochu Daveed and the children stayed only for a week in Madras after the funeral. He took them back to Kochi along with Susan and Jacob and handed them over to his mother to take care of them. He had to return to work as he had finished all his vacation days. All the members in Stephan's family did their best to help the children deal with the loss of their mother. Though it was their grandmother who took care of their food and shelter, they were somewhat sheltered psychologically by Susan and her siblings, who treated them like their own. Though the food was prepared in two different kitchens, they all ate together. They all prayed together and slept together in the big hall at the centre. They got adjusted to this new life. Only in the nights, Susan could hear the kids crying silently when they missed their mother.

Kochu Daveed was grateful for the all the help received from Stephan and his family. He wrote regularly to his eldest son, Joe, asking about their life in Kochi and sent him money for the monthly expenses of the whole family. Joe, who was fifteen years at that time, did his best to manage the expenses within the amount sent to him by his father. But there was always some sudden unexpected expense and so there was always a shortage by the end of the month. Because of this, he often borrowed some money from their neighbour, Chinna Chechi, and always returned it promptly when he received his money order of the month from his father.

Kochu Daveed's sisters visited them sometimes and they were not happy with the closeness Stephan and his family were enjoying with their brother's kids. They wrote to Kochu Daveed demanding him to send away Stephan and his family from the house and their next request was to consider marrying someone again. Kochu Daveed refused to accept both their demands. He said that his kids were very comfortable with Stephan and his family. He didn't want to disturb anything now. When they saw that he was not going to listen to them, they started pestering their mother to talk to Kochu Daveed about their demands when he comes to visit them next time.

When Kochu Daveed came for Easter holidays, his mother discussed this with him and though he refused to listen, she managed to make him understand that she is getting older and she may not be there always to take care of his children. He was in a dilemma. He didn't want to disturb the present conditions, but his mother would not leave him without a proper decision about the future. One day while going around his house he saw Susan all alone in their kitchen. He went in and asked her if she would be willing to become the mother to his children. Susan was stunned by this sudden proposal, but she recovered and said, "Achaya! I don't think that will work out. I love your children very much and they too love me. You are like a brother to me and I cannot think of you in any other way. I will take care of the kids as long as I am here. Your sisters don't like me and if you marry me, they will start the old rumours of an affair between us. You remember how Theresa Chechi was upset when she suspected that. So, please do not ask me to do this." Though Kochu Daveed was disappointed with her answer, he understood her logic and agreed not to ask her again. He told her not to disclose what he asked to anyone else. She promised to keep that a secret.

Next day he had a long discussion with his mother. He said he understood her anxiety and he asked her to give him some more time to settle everything. He said he planned to give a small plot of land from one corner to Susan for the help she and her family did to him. Once they build a small house in it and move there, he would start looking for another wife, just for the sake of the children. His mother accepted his decision and felt relieved that he had started thinking about the future.

After Easter he returned to Madras. Before going he had announced to Stephan about his plans of donating some land to Susan. Stephan was not very happy about it. He was expecting it in his name. But Marykutty, his wife, thought that it was a good idea and all others supported it. So, Stephan too agreed for that. While on the train to Madras, Kochu Daveed remembered his first train journey to Bombay and marvelled at all those events that had happened till this time. He closed his eyes and said a prayer of thanks to God for the strength he had given him to face all the situations in his life. He wondered how each small event was interconnected to take him this far in his life. He was not sure whether his decision to marry again was going to be a good one or bad. He knew that his intentions were good. He would try his best to make good of all the situations as before. He also knew that God would be with him always and he was ready to face the next Goliath and his only weapon was his belief in God.

-END-